A LITTLE HIDEAWAY

Celeste went out to join Dante on the wooden swing. The moon was full and the stars twinkled in the sky. The moon seemed brighter than normal as music filled the air.

"I love it down here," Celeste said, resting her head on Dante's shoulder. "It's so peaceful, so tranquil."

"Perhaps I should think of buying some property," Dante answered. "What do you think? Could you get used to this being our little hideaway?"

"I most certainly could," she said, standing. "You feel like taking a stroll?"

They walked hand in hand as moonlight guided their path away from the house. Celeste led Dante into the gazebo and motioned for him to take a seat on the bench as she stood before him, wedged between his legs.

"It's a lovely night," Celeste whispered as she leaned over him.

As Dante captured her lips with his, he had to agree.

SENSUAL AND HEARTWARMING
ARABESQUE ROMANCES FEATURE
AFRICAN-AMERICAN CHARACTERS!

BEGUILED   (0046, $4.99)
by Eboni Snoe
After Raquel agrees to impersonate a missing heiress for
just one night, a daring abduction makes her the captive of
seductive Nate Bowman. Across the exotic Caribbean seas
to the perilous wilds of Central America . . . and into the
savage heart of desire, Nate and Raquel play a dangerous
game. But soon the masquerade will be over. And will they
then lose the one thing that matters most . . . their love?

WHISPERS OF LOVE   (0055, $4.99)
by Shirley Hailstock
Robyn Richards had to fake her own death, change her
identity, and forever forsake her husband Grant, after testi-
fying against a crime syndicate. But, five years later, the
daughter born after her disappearance is in need of help
only Grant can give. Can Robyn maintain her disguise
from the ever present threat of the syndicate—and can she
keep herself from falling in love all over again?

HAPPILY EVER AFTER   (0064, $4.99)
In a week's time, Lauren Taylor fell madly in love with
famed author Cal Samuels and impulsively agreed to be his
wife. But when she abruptly left him, it was for reasons she
dared not express. Five years later, Cal is back, and the
flames of desire are as hot as ever, but, can they start over
again and make it work this time?

*Available wherever paperbacks are sold, or order direct from the
Publisher. Send cover price plus 50¢ per copy for mailing and
handling to Penguin USA, P.O. Box 999, c/o Dept. 17109,
Bergenfield, NJ 07621. Residents of New York and Tennessee
must include sales tax. DO NOT SEND CASH.*

MONIQUE GILMORE

Hearts Afire

PINNACLE BOOKS
KENSINGTON PUBLISHING CORP.

PINNACLE BOOKS are published by

Kensington Publishing Corp.
850 Third Avenue
New York, NY 10022

The P logo Reg. U.S. Pat. & TM Off. Pinnacle is a trade-
mark of Kensington Publishing Corp.

First Printing: July, 1995

Printed in the United States of America

This book is dedicated to my nephew,
Jalen Gilmore.
This one's for you, baby,
I LOVE YOU,
Aunt Monique.

One

Celeste Dunbar shut her eyes tightly allowing the teardrops to roll over her bottom lids. She didn't care about the black streaks of mascara trickling down her full cheeks. Quietly, she sniffed, reaching for a tissue. Glancing in the mirror, she studied her face for a moment. Her almond-shaped eyes were puffy and it was especially difficult to find those sparkling black eyes through her wet lashes. Refolding the tissue for the third time, she dabbed her cheeks, wiped under her eyes and reapplied her lip color. The coral lipstick accentuated her dark, mocha complexion. Besides, she needed something to lighten her mood and the bright lipstick was just the thing to do it, for now. *Funerals are always an emotionally draining experience*, she thought, tossing the tissue in the wicker trash basket.

The knock on the bathroom door was a clear signal that she had been in the tiny floral landscaped room too long.

"Just a second," Celeste said, quickly peeping into the mirror once more and running her fingers through her jet-black, short, vogue haircut. After checking to make sure her sideburns were still lying down neatly along her cheekbones, she opened the door. No one was standing on the opposite side of the door, which probably meant they could not wait any longer. The lyrics of Marvin Gaye and Tammy Terrel were muffled by sounds of loud laughter and mumbled conversations. Walking down the hallway that led from the bathroom, Celeste reached the top of the stairs. Upon her descent, she viewed the happenings around her, it was the typical after the burial and back to the house scene. People were scattered about wrapped in some type of black apparel; several strange faces gathered together. Paper plates were loaded down with foods ranging from fried chicken, blackeye peas, potato salad and collard greens to baked beans, string beans and pork chops. A group of unfamiliar faces were slouching on the worn burgundy velvet Queen Anne sofa. Celeste couldn't tell if it were the plates that were weighing down the sofa or the two huge women squeezing the small framed man.

"Hey there Little Bit. How you holding up?" Uncle Eddie asked Celeste.

"Oh, I'm hanging in there, Uncle E. How about yourself?"

"Girl, don't you go worrying about me. I'll be just fine. It's you everybody's worried about. Listen here Little Bit." He called her by her nickname. "If you need anything, I

mean anything at all don't hesitate to call your
Uncle Edward you hear?"

"I'm fine," she vowed, stretching up on her
toes to place a kiss on his cheek. Uncle Eddie
was a thick fair-skinned man standing 6'5 and
weighing more than 300 pounds.

Celeste excused herself as she continued to
nudge her way through the crowd towards the
back of the house. The large, country-style
kitchen painted a very different picture, but
familiar nonetheless. On the right side of the
kitchen was a counter parlayed with an assortment of vodka, gin, scotch, and rum, being
guarded, so it seemed, by a few slap-happy
relatives. Aunt Joyce, her husband Sammie,
Larry and his brother Joe were buzzing
around like they had just won the lottery. Aunt
Joyce, who always had a problem holding her
liquor, never had a problem finding it. *It was
obvious by her offbeat outfit: red skirt with a yellow
and lime green blouse, that Aunt Joyce had gulped
a few too many shots when she got dressed this morning,* Celeste thought smiling to herself. She
and Uncle Sammie's voices together were
louder than a cherry bomb exploding on the
Fourth of July. Although Celeste loved all her
relatives, there were some that she'd rather
love from a distance. She wished the distance
was much farther than the easy Washington,
D.C. commute where she lived, to the Alex-
andria, Virginia area where most of the Dunbar clan resided. On the left side of the
marble-rich kitchen stood Uncle Charlie, Aunt

Ruthie and Cousin Bobby arguing about "who
the hell should pay the taxes on granny's land
this year." The dispute was temporarily halted
by Celeste's presence. Cousin Bobby, a petite
man, sucked his yellowish teeth, twirled the
toothpick around in his mouth and greeted
Celeste. "Hey girl, come on over here and give
your old cousin Bobby a hug."

At first, Celeste stood frozen. She never
cared for Cousin Bobby or his over extended
hugs. He reminded her of a dirty old man
because he always made a habit of implying
that if they weren't related, he would give her
a run for her money. In addition to that, the
infamous Bobby Dunbar was an antiquated su-
perfly with a short man's complex.

Cousin Bobby's persistency was another annoying trait. He called out her name again.
Realizing that everyone in the kitchen had focused their attention on Cousin Bobby's request, Celeste, irritated as usual, conceded
and greeted her cousin with an A-frame hug.

"How the hell ya been sugar?" Cousin
Bobby asked in his fast talking voice.

"Fine. Thanks."

"Good, good," he said eyeing her up and
down. "Boy I tell you, you're getting prettier
and prettier every time I see you. When you
going to settle down and have some babies,
girl? You know, at the rate you're going you
ain't never going to catch up to your cousin
here," he bragged while thumping his chest.
"You know, Felicia just kicked out another one

for me last month. She named him after me, of course," he grinned.

"Of course," Celeste responded dryly.

"Bobby, hush your mouth for a minute and catch your breath," Aunt Ruthie chimed in. "Celeste, don't pay him no attention. You know how he's always spouting off about something he shouldn't. Celeste, you're looking a little frail around the ribs. You sure you're okay?"

"Yes, Aunt Ruthie. I'm okay, really. I wish everyone would stop worrying about me. Everything will be all right, I promise." If anything, Celeste was worried about the alcohol intake of her relatives and their future attempts to drive home.

"All right sweetie," Aunt Ruthie said kissing Celeste on the forehead. "I know how full of pride you can be and we just want to let you know we are here for you if you need anything."

Celeste glared down at the floor and nodded her head up and down a few times. She could feel the tears pushing up against the back of her eyeballs again. Not wanting to break down in front of her relatives, she politely excused herself and headed up the spiral staircase to the second level of the beautiful, two-story brownstone.

At the top of the stairs, she flipped on the hall light although she was familiar with the old house. She knew every nook and cranny of the hand-carved banister, every sound of the squeaky hardwood floors and every whistle of the wind whipping through the crescent-shaped windows. Celeste was no stranger to the trinket-filled house on Tennessee Avenue in Northwest Washington. After all, this was the house that cuddled her when she was a child, that warmed her with its marble fireplace when she was cold, that shielded her with its sturdy insulation when she was frightened, that expanded to about twelve rooms instead of a mere seven to accommodate her many slumber parties, and that welcomed her first date at the bottom of the brick steps. Indeed this house overwhelmed Celeste with memories.

She made her way to the master bedroom where she shifted the massive lump of coats and hats from the queen-size, four-poster, mahogany bed to the chaise lounge in the far corner of the room. The room was stuffed with antique furnishings, two Oriental throw rugs and an array of glass figures and hand-made dolls strategically aligned throughout. At the foot of the bed was an enormous oak chest filled with pictures, letters, books and silk scarves. On the vanity, there were fifteen perfume spray bottles neatly positioned atop the cream linen mat.

She looked around the antique-white and peach-colored room, kicked off her shoes, stepped onto the small foot stool and climbed on top of the bed. So much had happened during the past few days that she couldn't remember the last time she had some sleep. Tossing and turning for several minutes, Celeste finally sat up. Her mind was still racing and would not relinquish authority over to sleep. Perhaps what she needed was a brisk walk around the neighborhood a few times, she thought springing up from the bed. Then, maybe she would be able to relax enough to fall asleep.

Straightening her dark green dress, Celeste slipped her shoes back on. Making her way down the stairs, she bumped into a few more familiar faces. She acknowledged the gentleman on the far side of the room with a head nod and proceeded towards the front door. The gentleman waved for Celeste to stop but she was already out the front door.

On the front porch, the wooden benches and two oak rocking chairs were occupied by more relatives. Ms. Hattie, the next door neighbor, was leaning over the right side of her porch talking to Uncle Deak as he sat on the edge of the porch banister.

"Where you going sugar plum?" asked Uncle Deak in a somber tone.

"I'm just going for a walk. I need to clear my mind, that's all," Celeste replied.

"Why don't you get one of your cousins or someone to go with you? What about your friend there in the house, can't he go with you?"

"Stop worrying so much, Uncle Deak. I'm a big girl. If I need you, I'll yell. Besides, I'm only going around the corner."

Uncle Deak didn't say another word. He just

looked at her and shook his head. Celeste was always so independent and strong willed that all her relatives knew just to let her do her thing. He, of all people, knew first hand how stubborn his little niece could be. Four years ago, they had a heated discussion about whether she should pursue a career as a dentist or keep her job with the government while attending graduate school to get her Master's degree. The way Uncle Deak saw it, since he helped Celeste get the job starting at a Grade Level 11, she should hang in there and get her MBA. Then she could move up to a G-13 or G-14. But, Celeste wouldn't hear of it. Her mind was set and she would stop at nothing to follow her own dreams. In fact, she raised such a fuss about her decision to become a dentist that it nearly caused a split in the family. Uncle Deak was the first to drop the subject and eventually, the dust settled between them. Naturally, he wasn't going to push her about grabbing a chaperon just to walk around the block. The little neighborhood on the northwest side of Tennessee Avenue was relatively safe.

Celeste draped her wool jacket shut over both arms, bounced down the stairs, unlatched the tiny black wrought iron gate and veered right. Part way up the street, she could hear, from a distance, a car hurling around the corner on two wheels. The sound reminded her more of a high-speed police chase or a drag race than a normal drive. Whistling a popular tune, Celeste finally reached the corner. The screeching tires and revving engine were getting louder. Looking to her left, then to her right, Celeste stepped off the curb onto the street— just as a black, four-door sedan with tinted windows skidded to an abrupt stop in front of her.

Two big, round-faced white men jumped out of the back car doors. Celeste stood stiff as a board as panic started to kick in. Her heart was thumping faster than the wings of a bird lifting off for flight.

"Celeste Dunbar?" bellowed one man.

"Yes," Celeste responded with a puzzled look on her face. "Who wants to know?"

Before she had time to yell for help, both men had her by each arm. The taller man had poked the cold, metal object in her side, tightened his grip around her biceps and said, "Just keep walking. Don't say a word and everything will work out fine. Open your mouth, and you'll be laying here on the corner. Now get in the car!"

"What? Wait a minute! Who are you guys?" she said resisting their hold as best she could. "Hold on a second! There's been a mistake. I don't know who you guys are or what you want but I assure you I don't have it and don't want nothing to do with you."

"Shut up!" threatened the man on the left side of her as he tossed her in the back seat of the car and slammed the door. There were a few passers-by and neighbors on the porch watching Celeste being hauled off. The car sped off down the narrow street, tires turning the corners screaming like a race car driver. Celeste flopped to one side of the car as the car swerved around the corner. She was suffocating with fear and confusion. *Who are these people and what do they want with me?* She tried to remain calm.

"Here." The man on the left reached into his pocket and pulled out a piece of black cloth. He handed Celeste the cloth. "Put this over your eyes. And don't dare think about removing it either. It's still not too late to dump you in the Potomac."

Celeste didn't argue with the man. She just did as she was directed and placed the rough material over her eyes. Then, no sooner than she tied the piece of cloth around the back of her head, she felt the man on the right place a cup in her hand. "Drink this. We've got a little ride ahead of us. This won't harm you, it'll only make you drowsy."

Celeste didn't move. She held onto the cup but made no effort to raise it to her lips. Finally, after about thirty seconds, she felt the same cold, metal object pressed against the side of her cheek. Quickly she slammed the drink down her throat and dropped the cup on the floor. Whatever was in the cup made her throat burn. She could feel the effects taking over her body as she fought hard to keep from dozing off. But her will power was not as strong as the drug. She was beginning to slip into a coma-like freeze. Nodding her head forward then back in a last attempt to fight off the effect of the drink, Celeste's head slammed back against the back seat of the car.

Two

Earlier that year . . .

Alvin Brouchard jumped up out of the gray, tweed-colored ergonomic chair and stretched his long arms to the ceiling. Then he reached down and tapped his toes. Removing the tiny round framed glasses from his face, he wiped his forehead with a paper towel. The humidity was about to choke him to death. Last he heard, the temperature was 90 degrees with 100% humidity. He was sure most of the folks in the D.C. area were either coming from an air-conditioned environment or on their way to one. Walking from the small dining area to the L-shaped kitchen, Alvin began rummaging through the white-washed oak cabinets, in search of some energizing eatables. Not finding anything particularly appealing, Alvin let out a sigh. He had spent the last three hours plugging away at his computer before acknowledging his stomach's cry. At this point, a glass of ice cold water would be a welcomed treat. Unfortunately, there weren't any ice cubes in the ice tray and no clean glasses in the cabinet.

"Damn," he mumbled, slamming the cabinet shut. Celeste had asked him to start the dishwasher before she left for class, but as usual, he forgot. She was so particular about waking the neighbors, that it was an unspoken house rule that the dishwasher and stackable washer and dryer were not to run their cycles before 9:00am. Alvin didn't care about the neighbors one way or the other. If it were up to him, he would run the dishwasher at 3:00 am just to spite the next door neighbor, who had an annoying tendency to thump his bass from sunrise to sunset.

Since Pizza Hut had served as his main entree the night before, Alvin decided that he would step out and grab a bite at French's soul food restaurant. He couldn't remember the last time Celeste had whipped up one of her fancy dinners for him. When Celeste failed to receive a measly 2.5 carat ring at Christmas, it seemed she had done less and less for him and the household. The relationship had taken a spinning nose dive and hadn't been the same since. It was their most recent episode when Celeste vociferously expressed her unhappiness with his lack of commitment. She then accused him of being self-centered, greedy and materialistic.

Alvin really couldn't understand what all the fuss was about. The only thing he did was take his full month's paycheck, along with a

sizable amount of his savings, and invest in an
entrepreneurial opportunity that could have
made him financially free—had it worked. Perhaps spending $9400 on a get rich adventure
without paying any of the household expenses
was a bit much. But what other choice did he
have? He had to take the risk. The opportunity seemed too good to pass up. In retrospect,
it wasn't such a bright idea. Not so much because the opportunity failed, but because his
drive for money forced Celeste to borrow
money from her grandmother so that they
could pay the rent for two months.

Unhappy with their situation and weary
from all the battles, Alvin finally told Celeste
to pack her things since she seemed to be so
miserable.

The telephone rang, snapping Alvin back
from his reverie. He hesitated for a moment
trying to guess who could be on the other end
of the line. Maybe it was Celeste calling to tell
him that she would be out late studying with
some friends. Or, perhaps it was any man's
nightmare—Celeste's grandmother, NaNe, calling to needle him. Clearing his throat, he
picked up the cordless phone and said, "This
is Alvin."

There was no sound on the other end. Seconds elapsed between him and the raspy voice
that eventually became audible. "Is that the
way you greet your callers now? I'm sure
everyone knows your voice, Alvin. Anyway, is
Celeste there yet?"

"No," Alvin answered rolling his eyes up towards the ceiling. *Who in the heck does this woman think she is calling here talking to him like she was his mama?* he frowned.

"Well, what time do you expect her? Did she mention anything about coming over here when she got out of school?"

"I don't know what time she'll be back. Or, whether she's planning to stop by after class."

"You mean to tell me you two live together and you don't know what time she's supposed to get in from her lessons?"

Alvin didn't respond. He could feel his blood pressure start to rise and knew it would be better for him not to reply than to say something he should later regret, but more than likely wouldn't.

"Since the cat's got your tongue Alvin, tell Celeste to phone me when she gets home. Do you think you could remember that, or should I call back and leave a message?"

"Yes. I'll tell her," he said, irritated. She hung the phone up without saying good-bye. Something he found to be very rude for a woman of her caliber. He hated the way she talked down to him. All he ever did was once forget to give Celeste a message that NaNe had called and she never let him live it down. The only other thing he did was not marry her little granddaughter before moving her into his humble abode.

"That woman definitely has something coming to her one day," he muttered locking the door behind him. Now for sure he could use an "ice cold one" to help smooth the wrinkles out of his forehead.

He had lost his appetite for soul food and decided to swing by the local reggae joint down the way. When he entered, Bob Marley's "No Woman No Cry" was rolling out of the suspended JBL speakers. Immediately, Alvin could feel his anxiety and irritation float out of him. Bobbing his head up and down to the rhythm, he softly sang, "No woman no cry, No woman no cry." His eyes were shut tight as he stood in the middle of the floor moving his head and his hips to the contagious reggae beat. The women sitting at the table near the bar smiled to themselves as they focused their attention on Alvin's lanky 6'3 body. His gyration resembled a giraffe trying to swing a hula hoop around its neck.

Alvin was already intoxicated by the music when he finally reached the long, maple, horse-shoe-shaped bar. The small bar was buzzing with college students, business folks and a few neighborhood regulars. It was amazing how given the right atmosphere, coupled with some reggae music, everyone seemed to mix no matter what the race or religion. Pulling up a stool, Alvin sat with his back facing the bar. He wanted to do some people watching before placing his order. In the back of the bar, he noticed two Europeans in their early twenties playing a game of pool with a young Jamaican and an Asian. His best guess was that the guys attended either George Washington University or George-town University. On the left side of the bar over by the jukebox, he noticed a Lebanese couple wrapped in heavy discussion with an African brother. Bob Marley's "Get up, stand up, stand up for your rights" was now humming in the background.

"Excuse me brother, what will it be this evenin'?" asked the well-built, dark man in a thick Jamaican accent.

Turning around, Alvin smiled and answered, "I'll have the jerk chicken, potato balls and a glass of Sorrel. Where's Trevor tonight?"

"Him had ta go up north to New York to see him sister. Whom I tell him askin'?"

"Alvin man," he said standing then shaking his hand.

"Cool mon. I'm John. I take good care of ya. Be seated."

Alvin sat down with his back still facing the bar. How he wished he was still in college as he glimpsed over to the three young ladies sitting at the booth. They were apparently working on an assignment for school because papers were scattered all over the table and their eyes never left the pile of information lying before them. *Must be engineering or computer majors,* he quickly summarized. They had the kind of concentration that only a discipline such as engineering, math or computers could teach someone. Perhaps he should go over and introduce himself. Yeah, he could hear his spiel now.

Hi, I'm Alvin Brouchard, graduate of Georgetown University's Engineering program, class of 1984. You all look like you need some help. I'm sure I can solve whatever the problem is for a small fee. After all, I did graduate with honors. Why don't you slide on over and allow the chief to give you that peace you've been searching for. He had to snap out of the dream as John tapped his shoulder.

"Ere ya go, bro."

"Thanks man. Can I get some hot sauce?"

"Sure thing," John said handing him the bottle of Jamaican hot sauce. Alvin tore into the chicken like a man who had been on a fast. He slurped down the flower drink after each bite. Sorrel was an acquired taste, one he had developed during his teens in his last foster home. His foster parents, Mattie and Ron Desmond, were originally from Jamaica. Naturally, he grew up in the tiny house inhaling, ingesting and digesting the best curry chicken, gumbo, jerk chicken and fried plantain in the state.

Mattie and Ron decided they would return to Jamaica after Alvin graduated from high school. Their decision left Alvin to decide to either remain in the States, work and attend college, or move to Jamaica with them. Alvin chose to stay in the nation's capital and follow his dream to collect the dead presidents, as he liked to call dollar bills.

After attending a two year junior college in Maryland, he got accepted to Georgetown University. It also helped that he had befriended Tony Lucero, a fellow student at the junior college he played ball with from time to time.

Tony's family had connections. After a few weekend visits to Tony's parents' home in Annapolis, Alvin was soon regarded as a good friend of the family. It was the weekend of the NCAA final four tournament and Duke was battling for the title once again. Tony invited Alvin to attend a party to watch the game at his Uncle Franchesco's two million dollar mansion in Annapolis. It wasn't until the ride home that Tony shared with Alvin that his uncle was the "notorious" leader of the Gumichi family.

Uncle Franchesco told Tony that he would be willing to help Alvin if he ever got in a bind. Perhaps it was to Alvin's benefit that Franchesco Gumichi had been an orphan as well. And so the story all began with Franchesco using his contacts to help further Tony and Alvin's chances of getting accepted to Georgetown University's engineering program.

Wiping his lips with the napkin, Alvin tossed the paper on his plate and summoned John.

"I'll have a Heineken," Alvin stated. John nodded and headed back down to the end of the bar. Alvin could feel someone standing directly behind his stool. In fact, they were standing a little too damn close for his taste. Cocking his head over his left shoulder in one smooth swing, he let out a hearty laugh. "Hey Tony, what's up? Man I was beginning to wonder who that was walking up on me like that. What are you doing here?"

Tony grabbed Alvin's right hand and shook it tightly. "I knew I'd find you here rocking to some reggae. Didn't you get my message I left for you yesterday?"

"Naw man. Did you speak to Celeste or leave it on the machine?"

"I gave the message to Celeste. What? She didn't give it to you?" Tony asked raising a brow.

"Obviously not," snapped Alvin.

"What's up with you two? She still planning on moving out?"

"Yeah, that's what she says. But so far it's been a bunch of hot air. Supposedly she's been looking for a place but I haven't heard no more about it. You know what man?" Alvin paused taking a sip of his beer. "I'm tired of playing daddy. And, on top of that, I have to put up with her grandmother's rude behavior while she sits by and does nothing," he belched out. "If she wants out then she's got it. I'm not ready for marriage yet anyway. So, Tony what you drinking?"

"The usual. Listen Al, things will work out for you one way or another. They always do. Don't even sweat it," Tony smiled squeezing Alvin on the shoulder.

Alvin ordered the drink, purposely overlooking Tony's last remark. "What was the message you left for me?"

"Uncle Franchesco invited us out to the house this weekend. He said he had a business opportunity we might be interested in. Supposedly, he and a few of his partners need a couple of engineers to help figure out something. I don't know all the details yet, except that it could be financially rewarding."

"You know me Tony. I'm game if it's about the green."

Tony gulped down the shot of tequila and slammed the glass on the bar counter. "I'm out of here Al. I'll swing by and pick you up on Saturday around 12:15pm. Cool?"

"Fine. I'll see you then," Alvin said shaking Tony's hand again. He watched Tony make his way towards the exit door as he disappeared into the smoke. The bar was getting crowded and noisier, and the smoke more intense. Alvin reached into his back pocket and pulled out the cowhide wallet. He threw a twenty spot on the counter for the bill. What the heck, he smiled throwing a ten spot up on the bar as well. With any luck, he hoped silently, as he strolled towards the front door, this meeting with Franchesco Gumichi could be the money tree he had been searching for.

Celeste entered the foyer of the brick brownstone hanging her leather backpack over the banister. The onion, garlic and pepper aroma floating from the kitchen was a common scent. No matter what time of day Celeste's grandmother, NaNe, could be found standing over the stove.

"NaNe?" Celeste called cutting through the dining room into the kitchen. As long as Celeste could remember, she always referred to her grandmother, Urma Dunbar, as NaNe.

"Little Bit, I didn't hear you come in. How long you been here?" NaNe asked walking toward Celeste. She had on a floral apron that wrapped her large hips. Brushing her hands on the front of the apron, NaNe extended her arms towards Celeste while Celeste fell into the embrace kissing her grandmother on the cheek.

"You're looking too tiny Celeste," NaNe frowned while studying her granddaughter's petite frame. "What's wrong? Alvin can't afford to keep you nourished?"

Celeste turned her head in annoyance. NaNe made it painfully obvious that she didn't care for Alvin. Ignoring NaNe's intended insult, Celeste snatched an orange out of the wooden fruit bowl and sat down at the kitchen table. "What you cooking NaNe?"

"If you stay for dinner, you'll find out soon enough. Did that boy tell you I called?"

"Alvin?"

"Who else," NaNe replied banging the spoon against the pot trying to clear the contents off the spoon. "I can't help it, sugar. I raised you like my own daughter and I just want what's best for you. I'm of the belief that living with

a man who is not your husband is not going to
get you down the aisle any quicker. Your generation is cruising in the fast lane straight to
hell. Ms. Hattie was just telling me that her
niece is moving in with her boyfriend so they
can save some money. Personally, I wouldn't live
nowhere but home if I had to struggle with
some man who had a different last name than
me. No sir! I would have to make it on my own
or stay at home and save my money. Until, I met
a good man who could care for me enough to
make me his wife. You've got too much going
for you Celeste. You're beautiful, intelligent,
warm, good-spirited and classy. Why are you
settling for less? You know you could always
move back home and go to school," NaNe said
turning toward Celeste with a raised eyebrow
waiting for a response.

Celeste kept silent about her plans to leave
Alvin in the next couple of weeks. She had to
steer clear of NaNe's persuasive abilities. If
she wasn't careful, NaNe would have her back
home in her old room in the thump of a heartbeat. Celeste knew, just as Alvin did, that their
union was over.

The one thing she was certain of was that
she wouldn't miss Alvin and his greedy ways
all that much once she moved. The other thing
she was sure of was that the old wise tale about
not really knowing how a person is until you
live with them is true gospel. She imagined
that she might miss snuggling up to someone
every night, feeling warm and secure wrapped

in someone's arms and being able to be physically satisfied whenever she pleased. However, the tension between them had mounted to great new heights over the past several weeks. With Alvin's perpetual quest for material pleasures, in addition to his sloppy living habits and self-centered ways, Celeste needed out of their relationship. This relationship was too demanding, too time-consuming, and required a great deal of sweat and tactical maneuvers.

Celeste took another bite of her orange. "Come on NaNe. We've already been over this several times. For almost two years to be exact."

"That's exactly my point! It's been two years and still," NaNe paused picking up Celeste's left hand. "No ring. And for what? So you can keep his ugly toes warm at night?" She huffed dropping Celeste's hand.

"How did you know Alvin's toes are ugly?" Celeste giggled.

" 'Cause I know these things," NaNe replied pinching Celeste on the left cheek. Then NaNe let out a deep laugh and Celeste was relieved. She never did learn how to handle her grandmother's lectures, comments or just plain nagging about her life with regards to Alvin. She respected NaNe too much to hurt her feelings or say something distasteful. It was becoming almost unbearable living in the middle of NaNe and Alvin's war path. Alvin always accusing NaNe of trying to control her life. And NaNe always preaching about Alvin not respecting Celeste enough to make her an honest woman. What she had suggested on several occasions was for the two of them to hammer out their differences once and for all. But then she was sure that someone's feelings would inevitably be destroyed.

They exchanged a few more words over dinner before Celeste gathered her things to leave. Standing in the hallway glaring at the family photos on the wall, Celeste thought to herself: *It's a shame how children are forced to grow up and become adults. Why can't we cleave our parents' bosoms a little longer before stepping out into the cruel world?* Hanging out at NaNe's house meant you would be relaxed by the time you departed. Mainly because NaNe had a wonderful gift for making everyone feel at home when they came to visit her. Her hospitality rituals were simple. She would say to folks, "Come on in, sit down, rest your soul, have a bite to eat and something to drink and let's talk."

Talking was what NaNe was known for throughout her life. She grew up the eldest child of five in Augusta, Georgia. Having to plow the field and tend to her younger siblings, left NaNe with little opportunity to attend school. Her story was similar to so many Black Americans who migrated North from the South. NaNe's long and hard struggles were evident with stories that would make anyone cry. NaNe's hard life prepared her to be the wise, financially independent, successful woman she was now.

NaNe was sixteen when she met Edward

Dunbar, a tall handsome twenty-one year old, at the annual church picnic. In a matter of weeks, the two fell passionately in love, married and relocated north to Washington, D.C. Edward, "Doc" as he was known to many, worked as a carpenter in the Washington and Virginia area while NaNe got her high school diploma. Doc believed in Booker T. Washington's principle of education and that it was the only key to any kind of freedom. In fact, Doc cherished the educational system so much, he pushed NaNe to continue with her schooling until she received her BA in Education. Doc never complained about the fifteen hour days, six days a week he had to work just to keep food on the table or pay for NaNe's school books. Things were hard for them during those times. There were many nights when sardines and grits or hot dogs and beans served as their supper. Sometimes money got so tight, NaNe had to study by candlelight because they were unable to pay the gas and electric bill.

Once NaNe received her degree and landed a job teaching at a local elementary school, Doc cut back his work hours so that he could get his high school diploma. After one year and three months, Doc got his diploma. He continued his education and received an AA degree in Electronic Engineering and started his own TV, radio and stereo repair business, which became extremely successful and well-known throughout the D.C. area.

During his last year at the junior college, NaNe, who was twenty-five years old, gave birth to their first and only child, Lorraine. For years, the Dunbar trio did well financially. They invested in property, took small family vacations and sent several hundreds of dollars back home to help less fortunate family members. Doc moved a few of his brothers to Washington giving them jobs in his business.

The Dunbar clan was sailing along smoothly for twenty years with no major dilemmas— until the day Lorraine came home from college pregnant. Although, NaNe admitted to Lorraine that Stanley Jones was a "handsome devil," that's all that he was. A devil who left Lorraine standing at the altar devastated and heartbroken. This incident, in addition to the shameful pregnancy, left Lorraine feeling withdrawn and depressed. NaNe and Doc showered Lorraine with as much love and support that she would let them. But the support Lorraine was receiving from her parents was not enough.

After Celeste was born, Lorraine quickly indulged in a life of partying and drinking in an attempt to escape from the pain of being rejected by Stanley and of being an unwed mother. Well, fate would have it that Stanley was drafted to fight in the Vietnam War, where he would later lose his life. Lorraine, after a bout of drinking one night, drove her car off the Chesapeake Bay Bridge. Both NaNe and Doc were crushed over Lorraine's death. They spent many nights and days speculating over whether there was anything they could have done to save their daughter.

After several months, the dark cloud that covered the Dunbar family began to lift. They realized that there was still a Dunbar trio and that they had another chance to help mold another life, Celeste's. From that day forward, Celeste helped to fill the void.

Staring at her grandmother with an intent gaze exuding thank you and I love you, Celeste grinned. NaNe was her best and loyal friend and the only mother she'd ever known. No one understood their relationship. How could she blame her grandmother for wanting the best for her?

Celeste snapped a mental picture of her grandmother's physique. She wondered if she would develop those wide Matisse hips after childbirth. She had even inherited her smooth, soft, dark complexion and thick, jet black hair.

NaNe called out Celeste's name a second time before Celeste realized that she had been engulfed in a time warp.

"Celeste, I know I can be hell on wheels sometimes sugar. But, I just want what's best for you. I don't want you to make any costly mistakes. That's all."

"I know NaNe," she smiled placing her arm around NaNe's waist.

"There's something about Alvin that rubs me the wrong way and always has. I have prayed and prayed about it but I can't lay my finger on it. He's got two sides to him and we only know half. Just be careful," she warned shaking her head slightly. "Just be careful."

"I will NaNe, I promise. Don't worry. The same God you pray to is the same one I know," Celeste said opening the front door. "God will look after me," she said in a somber tone. "He always does."

Three

"You're so ungrateful Alvin. That's your problem," Celeste protested shaking her finger at Alvin. "You are overly concerned with what Alvin wants and what Alvin needs that you never consider anyone else."

"I wouldn't say that so fast Celeste," Alvin huffed under his breath. "I seem to recall having your best interest at heart when you moved in here." He was carrying a small box and pushing another one with his foot. "What is the real issue, Celeste?"

"You don't respect me enough to share in the household duties. You don't care enough to prove you love me. You don't love me enough to propose marriage to me. The only person you care about is yourself."

"Kill it with the drama Celeste. You act like I'm such a terrible person that twisted your arm to be here for the past two years. If anybody was looking out for themselves, I suggest you take a look at yourself," he fretted tossing the boxes in the back seat. "Sounds like your grandmother talking if you ask me."

"This has nothing to do with her or the

$1800 we owe her because of your irresponsible behavior." There, she finally said what was on her mind.

"If it's about the damn money, I can go to the bank and get a loan to repay your grandmother. You would think she'd give us more than two measly months to pay her back." He was furious now. How dare she bring up the money issue, he frowned. He had intentions of repaying that old witch as soon as he got his bonus check next month.

"Just forget it Alvin," Celeste said leaning against the passenger door.

"Yeah let's do that. But you can tell your grandmother I will be mailing her a check as soon as I can."

Celeste let Alvin load the last two small boxes in the back seat of "Beauty," the nickname for her 1966 canary yellow Ford Mustang. Alvin was starting to make her stomach turn. Right now all she could think about was the tiny apartment that awaited her in the 200 unit residential complex in Arlington, Virginia. Her bed, dresser and sofa were scheduled to be delivered on Monday. All she had to deal with today were the boxes and her clothes.

Looking past Alvin, Celeste mumbled, "Thanks."

"Don't mention it," Alvin exhaled annoyed.

"Before I forget," she said digging in her purse and pulling out the key chain with the Howard University emblem on it. "Here are your keys."

Alvin grabbed the keys, stuffed them in his jeans and cleared his throat. "Guess this is it then."

Celeste felt stuck, confused about what her next sentence should be. *What should she say,* she thought. *Surely this isn't the way the chapter is supposed to end. Everything was going along a little too neatly. Wasn't this the part where Alvin professes his undying love for her as he pulls her to his chest? Where's all the mushy stuff? Why isn't Alvin following the script?* Perhaps she should quit watching so many old love stories, she thought shaking her head. Getting a grip on her thoughts, she gave him a tight hug. "Take care Mr. Brouchard."

"You too, Ms. Dunbar. Be safe." Alvin stood in the street, eyes following the red tail-lights until they disappeared. He felt a slight twinge in his stomach.

Celeste pulled into the narrow driveway scanning the buildings for the letter J. Maybe she had the wrong building letter. Circling the large complex once more, she sighted the J building off to the corner. The parking lot was swamped with cars crammed into every possible parking space. Someone had taken the liberty of parking in her assigned space, so she pulled behind the black Nissan 300ZX blocking the car in. She figured the only way to alert the neighbors that the new kid was in town and that her parking space was off limits was to barricade the intruder.

She was exhausted and felt like she looked worse than she felt. At least she could have put on some lip color or mascara to help create the illusion of a beautiful today. Her hair was matted, thanks to the Monarchs Negro league baseball cap she had clamped down on her head. Her shorts were stuck to her thighs and her tee-shirt damp with perspiration.

Carefully, she unloaded the box marked "fragile" on the small landing in front of her new home. *God I'm glad I chose the first floor apartment,* she thought, walking back to the car. She paused briefly, resting her hands on her hips, trying to decide what to unpack next. Overall, she had a small load in comparison to what someone who was more established than she would have. Leaning over into the back seat, she picked up the two boxes marked "stereo." Struggling to keep her balance, Celeste cautiously traced her steps back to the apartment door. This time a tall figure stood in her pathway, hustling to step out of her way. The boxes, which partially blocked Celeste's vision, were too heavy. She fought tooth and nail not to let them hit the ground. Moving quickly to Celeste's rescue, the tall figure reached out and caught the boxes. "Here, let me get these for you," came a deep voice.

Celeste released the boxes to the tall man standing to the side of her. "Thanks," she sighed. "I think I bit off a little too much."

"How come such a beautiful young lady is moving all this stuff by herself?"

"I don't know," Celeste said blushing. For the first time in a long while, she was at a loss for words. This man standing upright before her was absolutely, incredibly, gorgeous.

"Dante Lattimore," he said softly extending his right hand.

"Celeste Dunbar," she smiled cupping his hand. "Nice to meet you."

His hands were soft like a satin sheet and his skin was a rich, golden-brown color. Simply put, Celeste had been taken aback by Dante. Everything about him was tailored, from his nails to his defined hairline. Even his thick eyebrows and long eyelashes, highlighting his large brown eyes, knew their place. His cream linen suit fell perfectly and the brown, hand-woven, Italian strapped sandals matched perfectly. *Oh my Lord*, she gasped. *This could be an interesting situation developing here.*

Dante noticed Celeste investigating him and felt a smile rising inside. Doing a little inspecting of his own, Dante had to admit that Celeste had a natural beauty about her. Not many women could pull off a no make-up, baseball cap day and still be attractive. Besides, if there was anything to be said about a woman driving a 1966 original pony, then Celeste had the floor.

"This is a fine car. You've done a great job keeping it clean," Dante said reaching back into the car for another box.

"Thank you," she grinned reaching out to help him. She could feel her heart beating with excitement everytime she caught a glimpse of him.

"No, no. I've got it. If you want to do something special, how about unlocking your apartment door so we can put these boxes inside?"

Celeste moved toward the door in what seemed like one long leap. Once inside the apartment, she pulled the vertical blinds to the patio door open allowing the afternoon sun to filter in. Dante removed his coat and helped unload the few boxes from the car until all the boxes were stacked neatly in the living room corner.

"Whew. It's hot out there," he said wiping his face with the back of his hand.

"I know. I wish I had something to offer you to drink or a seat to offer you."

"Don't worry about it Celeste," he exhaled. "Have you had anything to eat yet?"

His invitation caught her by surprise. Perhaps she felt as though he was reading her mind because she wanted to find a reason to linger in his presence a little longer. "No I haven't," she lied.

"I know this little place down the hill if you're up for it."

"Sure," she said smiling widely. "But first I need to freshen up a bit. How about you meet me back here in twenty minutes?"

"You only need twenty minutes? That'll be a first for me," Dante smirked.

"Well, the clock is ticking. Now, I'm down to nineteen minutes. Believe me Dante, I'll be ready in eighteen."

"Yeah, okay. We'll see," he said walking out the door.

As soon as Dante shut the door, Celeste grabbed her duffle bag and quickly located her toiletries. Having removed the hat off her head, she realized how matted her hair was. "What to do, what to do," she whispered. Wetting the brush, she applied some gel on her hair then took the bristle brush and slicked it back off her face. Then she took a fast birdbath. "Seven more minutes," she said rifling through her bag trying to find something to put on that didn't require ironing. Finding the peach, cotton sun dress still in a fairly pressed state, she slipped it on. Then she slid her feet into her three-inch summer mules. "Three more minutes," she said rushing back into the bathroom where she applied some coral lipstick and perfume.

The knock on her living room door came promptly at the twenty minute mark. Dante stood with his back to the door waiting for Celeste to answer. He was sure that she wasn't ready yet. But when she opened the door and he saw that she was fully dressed and looking radiant, his mouth fell open.

"I don't believe it," Dante grinned.

"I told you I'd be ready," she smiled batting her eyes. Dante backed away from the doorway in order to allow Celeste to get out. She picked up her purse, locked the door then turned and walked with Dante down the pathway.

"Do you mind if we take your car since some-one," he paused looking at Celeste then point-ing to his car, "has blocked me in." They both let out a soft laugh and proceeded to Celeste's car.

They arrived at the tiny cafe in no time. The atmosphere was warm, pleasant and quaint. There were only five tables in the entire shop plus a small counter with six bar stools. Dante led her to a table in the back of the cafe.

"Is this okay?" he asked.

"This is fine, Dante," she smiled.

Dante pulled out her chair for her while she took a seat. Once she was seated he waited to see if she needed to adjust her chair before taking his seat.

"Thank you," she said.

"You're perfectly welcome."

"So," she said picking up the menu. "What's good at this place?"

"Everything. But my favorite is the chicken salad with water chestnuts. It's got a spicy, curry taste to it. Do you like curry?"

"I love curry. I just wish I knew how to cook with it better."

"Yeah it's kind of hard to master the Car-ibbean flavors. Especially if you're not from one of the islands," he chuckled. "Do you like reggae music?"

"Love that too. Bob Marley is my all time favorite."

"Oh heck yeah. Nobody can outdo that man. He was brilliant and very spiritually gifted. It's too bad that most of our gifted brothers depart from us at such an early age. Look at Donnie Hathaway and Marvin Gaye. Those brothers still had a lot of life and messages to convey to the masses."

"I know. I was so sad when I heard that Marvin Gaye died. You know who else's death affected my heart?" she asked looking down at her napkin.

"Who?"

"Minnie Rippington. Nobody has been able to send chills through me like her."

"That's right. I almost forgot about Ms. *I stumbled on a photograph, it kind of made me laugh. . . .back down memory lane,*" he sang in his best rendition of Minnie Rippington's voice.

Celeste laughed and then shook her head. "I don't think you should give up your day job yet."

"You mean I can't sign up for the Apollo just yet?" Dante teased.

"Not quite yet. But do keep trying." They both let out peals of laughter.

At first, Celeste felt uncomfortable being in the company of such a handsome, polished, well-dressed man while she felt like she had just thrown herself together on short notice. But then after a few laughs, she no longer felt self-conscious about her appearance.

Dante couldn't believe how easily the conversation and laughter were flowing. He was trying hard not to stare at her while absorbing her natural beauty. Dante was sure Celeste caught him sneaking a peek at her when she wasn't looking. But too bad. The girl was gorgeous and very articulate, characteristics that were both hot buttons for him. Dante had to resist the urge to reach over the table and take a playful bite of her neck. She smelled so sweet he could have easily mistaken her for an exotic dessert of some kind.

They spent the next three hours at the little cafe eating and talking. Dante was well versed in a variety of subjects. The main topic of their discussion seemed to center around the issue of whether a high visible athlete should be considered a role model and held accountable for his indiscretions? Their views were similar, clashing occasionally depending on which athlete they were referring to.

"So what are you saying Celeste? That Michael Jordan shouldn't be allowed to engage in hobbies unbecoming to the public?" Dante said turning the palms of his hands toward the ceiling.

"No, that's not what I mean. I just feel that athletes have a responsibility to the very little people who have put some of them in the positions they're in."

"I understand what you're saying. But it's the role of the parents to instill morals within their children. Not the athlete."

"I don't see it that way Dante," she said

showing her disapproval by raising her eyebrows. "When an athlete is in the spotlight, portraying an image of a big brother or role model, there is a certain protocol that is attached. That's all I'm saying."

"I respect what you're saying but I still feel like it's nobody's business what an athlete does off the court or field if it doesn't harm anyone. If M.J. or L.T. want to gamble one hundred thousand dollars in a single roll of the dice, so be it. It's their money, they've taken enough blows to earn it," he said defensively.

Celeste detected the edge in Dante's voice and took a moment to gather her thoughts. "I get the feeling this is a sensitive subject for you," she grinned sideways.

He returned the smile and replied, "You could say that."

"Why is that?" she pushed a little more.

"Because I'm an assistant coach for a college basketball team in the area and have this discussion with the teachers and parents daily."

"I get the picture now," she said jerking her head back with surprise. "Well, I hope I haven't been too harsh. Then again, I am entitled to my opinion," she added, stirring her ice-tea.

"That you are," he answered. "But, I still feel that it's nobody's business what the greatest basketball player who ever played the game does with his money."

"The greatest basketball player to ever play the game?" she said tilting her head to the left. "You think Michael is a better player than Magic was?"

"Well, for this era, yes. I most certainly do."

"Get the heck outta here," she laughed. "Michael is all of that but Magic was a better teamplayer. A more rounded player overall."

Dante let out a broad smile. He found it amazing that a sister could hold her own when it came to the game. He stared at her a moment longer, then replied, "I see you know a little bit about the game. You must have some brothers or a boyfriend."

"No," Celeste responded smoothly. "It is only my grandmother and me. I just have a decent eye for the game. That's all. I don't profess to be an expert, but I do have some knowledge about the sport."

Lunch time had ended and the staff began to set the tables for the early evening crowd.

"Are you ready to go?" Celeste asked.

"Not really," Dante smiled. "I'm enjoying the conversation too much. I tell you what. Let me go home and get out of these clothes and I'll come over and help you unpack."

"Really?"

"Yes. Really. That's if you could use the help," he shrugged.

"I sure could," she said smiling from ear to ear. It startled Celeste that she could feel so comfortable and relaxed with this total stranger. Perhaps it was his full, uninterrupted attention to her every word that made her feel special. The feeling was similar to that of a dancer gracing the audience with her moves as each viewer looked on in awe. He studied her lips, her eyes and her body language the way an artist would his subject. He knew exactly what to say, when to say it and how to say it. Not once did he choke her sentence off with the beginning of his. And if he slipped and did cut her off, he would always excuse himself. Another thing she liked about Dante was his familiarity with such soothing but often forgotten words as *thank you, excuse me, pardon me* and *allow me*. She could feel her heart's pace quicken with each thought of Mr. Dante Lattimore. In fact, her heart and mind were skipping a little bit too fast for a first encounter. However, she had learned years ago to go with the flow of a natural thing instead of over analyzing it. If there was anything suspicious about Dante Lattimore, she was sure of one thing. God would let her know.

Dante arrived promptly at seven-thirty p.m. dressed in a pair of jeans shorts, a red polo shirt and a pair of leather sandals. To Celeste, it seemed like he was on his way to a barbecue because he looked so casual and smelled so good.

"Come on in and make yourself comfortable," Celeste said, inviting him inside. "I've already unpacked the kitchen boxes. I thought what we could do is set up my stereo, so at least, we could have some music. I took the liberty of ordering a pizza. I hope that's all right."

"You didn't have to do that, Celeste. But of course nothing sticks to your ribs like Italian," Dante joked slapping his stomach.

Celeste stood in the living room scanning Dante's profile once more. Seemed like nothing stuck to Dante's ribs or any other part of his body for that matter. To the best of her ability, she was able to get a good glimpse at his stomach and waist. His shirt had no difficulty staying tucked in his shorts. However, Dante was not to be mistaken for a frail brother. He obviously works extremely hard for his body's definition and is conscious about maintaining his framework, Celeste assessed quietly.

Within a matter of minutes, Dante had the stereo connected and the speakers buzzing.

"My God Celeste," he paused flipping through her albums, "I can't believe you still have all of these old albums. Music was at its greatest then. Look at this old stuff: Taste of Honey; Chaka Khan; GQ; Roy Ayers; Lonnie Liston Smith; Kool and the Gang; Earth, Wind and Fire; The BlackByrds; Parliament; Rick James; Switch; Michael Franks; Grover Washington Jr.; Al Jarreau; Cameo; Confukshun; Gap Band; Peabo Bryson; Stephanie Mills and the Spinners. Girl, you've stolen my heart for sure," he said in amazement.

"I don't believe it!" his voice raised picking up the album cover for closer inspection. "I've been searching all over for this John Lucien album on CD. Can I put this on?" His face was beaming like a kid on Christmas Day.

"Sure," Celeste replied. Dante had been swept away by the music collection and Celeste felt proud. She was happy that she held onto her albums and the Technic's turntable with the fine needle that cost her ninety dollars back in 1985. Sure she had to keep up with the times and eventually succumb to the world of Compact Discs. But, if she had her pickings, she would prefer the battle scars and scratches of Roberta Flack's "First Time Ever I Saw Your Face" any day over the clarity of the infra red.

Dante took great precautions to find the cheesecloth to wipe off the album then blow off the dust from the needle before letting her rip. John Lucien's *Gingy* came sliding out the speakers like a harpist ever so softly stroking her cord.

"God I remember this song like it was ten years ago. Can I have this dance lovely lady?"

Dante didn't bother to wait for a response. He reached out, took Celeste's hand delicately and gracefully whisked her around the tiny living room area. Celeste fell into a spirited trance savoring every step as she allowed herself to be shepherded about. She wanted the song to last forever. There was something special about being swept around the dance floor with your head and your heart pressed firmly in the secure bosom of a handsome man.

Before long, Dante and Celeste had rewound back to the past reminiscing about old times, old groups, old dances and old love songs. Rick James and Tina Marie's *Fire and Desire* were blaring out of the tiny but potent Cerwin Vegas speakers. They paused briefly only to answer the door and greet the pizza delivery girl. Without skipping a beat, their conversation played on just as the songs, skipping occasionally to grab another album. Time was not of the essence with regards to Celeste and Dante. The only noticeable hint to them that the hours had slipped by was the birds chirping in the background.

"It must be really late," Celeste said yawning.

"You mean really early, don't you?"

Celeste grinned and nodded her head. "What time is it anyway?"

Dante shrugged his shoulders, leaned back on the carpet resting on both his elbows and said, "I didn't wear my watch. Somehow I didn't really care about the time."

Celeste blushed, reached over and pulled her watch out of her purse. "Wow! It's four forty seven a.m. Can you believe that? We've been up talking for nine hours." She took a moment, gave a flashback smile and continued, "The last time I stayed up round the clock conversing to the multiple sounds of various artists was during my senior year in college. I still can't believe this."

"Neither can I. It's a good thing you don't have class tomorrow and I don't have a game because we would truly be some tired folks.

I'm almost too tired to walk home. Are there any laws prohibiting pedestrians from walking when they're intoxicated from sleep deprivation?"

"Not unless you live in California," Celeste said playfully touching Dante's hand. She could feel the attraction, the magnetic pull, drawing her closer. Dante could sense it too but suppressed the temptation.

"I best be making my long journey home," he said standing up. "Besides, I don't want to be caught creeping out of the new neighbor's house at this Godforsaken hour. It's like the old college days around here. You remember. When students would set their alarms first thing in the morning to catch a view of the night crawlers tip-toeing from one dorm to the next," he grinned.

"Well, we can't have that now can we?" she teased batting her eyelashes innocently. "I'm not really sleepy are you?"

"Not particularly. But I am hungry."

"Still?"

"I know you're not referring to those slices of pizza I ate five hours ago. You know how brothers are Celeste," he said throwing his hands up in the air. "If we're hungry, we'll eat. If we're not hungry, we'll eat."

Celeste laughed and shook her head. Why was she so attracted, so intrigued, so comfortable with Dante? What she wanted to suggest was that they shower, jump in the car and drive down to Maryland for an early fish and egg breakfast. But then she didn't want to seem too forward. She couldn't chance Dante getting the wrong idea about her sincere intentions.

"How about this," he pondered rubbing his thumb and pointer finger down his chin. "We jump in the hoopty and roll down to Maryland, as my players would phrase it, catch us a fish or two, fry it up right there and eat. I know this spot where they'll let you do that. What do you think?"

Celeste flinched, slightly stunned by Dante's gift to pick her thoughts. She let a confident smile creep across her face and softly replied, "I think you need to stop trespassing through my mind. Or, I'll have to start charging you an admissions fee."

"Is that right?" he said grabbing her by the waist, wrapping his arms around her back then pulling her within a few inches of his lips.

Celeste swallowed hard. She could feel her heart beginning to quicken its pace. Not wanting Dante to suspect how truly drawn she was to him, she eased out of his embrace. Although she would have preferred to linger in his hold a while longer. He smelled so good standing tall, pressing her head against the middle of his chest. She was glad that he didn't try to kiss her. Hell, his sweet breath and alluring voice were enough to kick start her heart. She didn't need a kiss to push it into overdrive.

"You driving?" she asked grabbing her purse.

"Only if you promise to be an alert co-pilot."

"Oh, I have a feeling that will not be a problem," she said confidently standing toe to toe with Dante, lips partly open. "I always make a good teamplayer."

My Lord, she thought. *It was only Saturday morning. How was she going to make it to Monday without being swept completely off this planet?* Easy. She would just have to slow the roll if it took off too rapidly.

Celeste and Dante had spent the rest of Saturday together, stopping to catch a movie before leaving the Maryland area to drive back to DC. Once Dante found out that Celeste was a fourth year dental student, he made jokes throughout the day about her being the only woman he'd let clean his teeth. Celeste told him she'd be more than happy to take a look inside his mouth. But for other reasons than he thought, she confessed silently. They both barely escaped the strong urge to seal their lips together Saturday night when Dante walked Celeste to her door.

Sunday was less challenging for Dante and Celeste because they both had previous engagements. Although, Dante did call Celeste Sunday evening to offer his assistance if she needed it before he turned in for the night. Celeste found it hard to resist seeing him but knew she had an early day in the morning.

Instead, they settled for a three hour conversation on the phone. They both thought it pretty silly considering they lived within a stone's throw away from one another. But there was something romantic, something special about being so close, yet choosing to communicate over the phone instead.

Dante was relieved that Celeste hadn't invited him to come over. It gave him a chance to get a better handle on the reasons why he felt so attracted to her, besides for the usual. He was being drawn to her like a fierce current. He would have to take it slow with Celeste, if he could help it. If not, he would just go with the flow.

Celeste arrived at HU's campus early Monday morning in the hopes of having time to settle in before her first patient arrived. She eased into her blue lab coat while walking into the large Russell Dixon Building. Clipping her ID onto the front pocket of her jacket, she was surprised to see Dante standing in the doorway of the clinic. He was casually decked out in a pair of navy slacks and a colorful cotton sweater. Although she fought desperately to refrain from exhibiting all thirty two of her teeth at her first glimpse of Dante, it was an effort in vain. Dante had definitely made her cheeks crease. Tucking her hands into the pockets of her lab coat, she continued to walk toward Dante.

"Good morning," he said, grinning.

"What are you doing here?" she asked.

"I was hoping I could get my teeth cleaned today," he said moving aside so she could get through the door.

"Really? Well, I'm flattered Dante but I can't work on your mouth without getting some X-rays and having you sign up with the clinic director." She walked over to her area of the clinic and placed her purse on the dental chair. She could feel Dante's eyes scanning her body and felt surprisingly shy. Turning around, she was shocked to see him sprawled out in one of the chairs with his mouth wide open. Celeste laughed.

"I'm serious Dante. I won't be able to clean your teeth today. But if you want to schedule an appointment, you have to get all the necessary paperwork done. And then we can go . . . from there. Besides, I have a patient arriving in just a few minutes."

Dante leaned further back in the chair and glared up at her in adoration. *Damn she's gorgeous!* He smiled looking her over from head to toe. She had on a printed sarong skirt that landed two inches above the knee and a matching silk top that buttoned down the front. The top two buttons were left undone exposing the thick herringbone necklace draped around her neck. Her blouse was tucked in at the waist highlighting her tiny hourglass shape. He could see how shapely her legs were as he gazed down at her suede two inch pumps. Feeling a surge of excitement shoot through his pants, he sprang up quickly. He didn't want Celeste to see the kind of effect she was having on him physically. Celeste turned away and walked back over to her side of the clinic. Dante watched her hips swing naturally underneath the lab jacket.

"Well, can I at least hang out for a while and learn a little more about crowns and cavities?"

Celeste smiled and nodded yes. "Only until my patient comes." *You can hang out here as long as you want my handsome brother,* she concluded silently.

Dante took a seat next to her chair and watched her every move as she began preparing for her patient. He studied her movements and facial expressions while she perused the vanilla folder.

Dante got a thrill out of watching Celeste perform her tasks and had to remind himself that he had only met this woman seventy two hours ago. At one point, he spotted the burgundy lace bra peeking through the silk top as she reached over to grab an instrument from the counter. She moved with such grace and ease that he found himself daydreaming about how soft she felt. Halting his thoughts abruptly, he had to admit the inevitable to himself. He could become very fond of her. So far, everything about this woman told him that he had to spend more time with her. Perhaps Dr. Dunbar would be the woman to finally capture his interest long enough to make him consider moving down a different road regarding relationships.

"Doctor Dunbar," Dante said smiling. "I was wondering if you'd like to come to my basketball game this evening? That's if you don't have other plans, of course."

"Are you coaching tonight?" she asked.

"Oh, no. The season hasn't started yet. This is just a recreational game with me and a couple of the brothers in the DC area. We get together once a week or so to vent our frustrations and see what kind of new cuss words we can create," he said smirking then hunching his shoulder. "I would really like it if you could come."

"What time is the game?" she said walking over toward the sink.

"Seven-thirty."

"I would love to," she smiled. "The furniture people are supposed to make a delivery at my apartment around five. I should have plenty of time. Where's it going to be?"

"At the main YMCA downtown. So," he paused, walking up behind her, "can I count on your applause for later?"

No, what this brother could do was back away from her before she reached out and grabbed him around the neck and planted a wet kiss on him, she thought to herself. After a few seconds of self-talk, Celeste replied, "You sure can." She turned around to face him, something she knew she shouldn't have done but it was too late. They were already standing inches away from each other. Thank God another fourth year student walked into the clinic just as Dante pressed his lips against hers. Dante immediately stepped back when he heard the clinic door open. He took a deep breath and let out a sigh, then said, "That was a close one."

"You're telling me," Celeste whispered. "You'd better go. I'll see you later tonight."

"Promise?"

"Promise," she said winking at him then turning her back and walking to the other side of the clinic.

Later that evening, Celeste arrived at the gymnasium promptly at 7:15pm. Dante's game was scheduled to begin shortly. She figured if the brother could come hang out with her at the clinic, the least she could do was come out and support him during his game. Members of the two teams were already warming up on the court when she walked in. The gym was sprinkled with an assortment of fans ranging from young to old, black and white, and men and women. This was the first time since her high school days that she would sit in the audience cheering for a special man, she thought. She skimmed the sidelines, careful not to walk on the court with her heels.

Dante caught a quick glimpse of Celeste as she tight-roped along the sidelines looking for a seat. "Hey beautiful," he smiled sneaking up behind her while bouncing the basketball. "Glad you could come out."

"Hello Dante," she grinned bashfully. "Looks like you guys have a lot of fans."

"Yeah. They're mostly the wives, girlfriends and children of the players. And there are some avid basketball spectators who just love a plain old street ball challenge between the brothers."

"So it seems," she said glancing around the gym once more. "Shall I wait for you after the game?"

"Please do," he winked jogging back over to his side of the court to join his teammates.

Celeste found a seat in the second row of the bleachers next to a woman and her son.

"Hello," the child said smiling widely.

"Hello," Celeste responded returning the warm smile.

"Who are you here to see?" the little boy, who was no more than six years old, asked.

"I'm here to see number seven," she answered pointing to Dante.

"Oh, the star!" the kid said with grave excitement. "That's Mr. Lattimore. He and my daddy are on the same team."

"Is that right?"

"Yup. That's my dad right there." The kid paused to point out his dad. "He's number fifteen. He's the guard on the team. Do you know what position Mr. Lattimore plays?"

"Not exactly," Celeste conceded.

"He plays forward. Do you know what that is?"

"Sure do. But maybe you could refresh my memory," Celeste said still smiling.

"What's refresh mean?"

"Jason don't bother the nice lady, all right?

She's trying to watch the game," his mother cut in flickering a half grin at Celeste.

"It's okay. I don't mind at all," Celeste beamed turning her eyes back to the kid. "So your name is Jason huh? Well, my name is Celeste."

"Nice to meet you Ms. Celeste," the kid said barely looking at her. His eyes were planted firmly on the players.

Celeste watched Dante as he warmed up with his fellow team members. She could tell right away that he was a gifted ball player that commanded an enormous amount of respect from his teammates. After a series of lay-ups and 15 footers, Dante and his team, all dressed in black, made their way to the bench. A few more minutes ticked off the clock before the horn sounded representing the start of the game. From what she could gather, there seemed to be no love lost between Dante and the opponent he was guarding. Twelve minutes into the game, Dante's team was leading the blue team by six points when the referee issued a time-out to the blue team.

Dante's body glistened as he huddled with his teammates to strategize about their opponents. Looking up and over to where Celeste was seated, Dante gave her another wink followed by a crooked smile as he twirled his mouthpiece in and out of his mouth with his tongue. She returned the wink and smile then shifted her look to Jason, who was yelling for his dad to do a dunk for him. As Dante slowly strolled back onto the court, Celeste took the opportunity to check out his body some more. He had on a pair of baggy sweat shorts that fell right above the knees and a sleeveless tank top that exposed the hair on his tightly cut chest. His legs were hairy too, something she found to be sexy. He had well developed calves and tight biceps. She even found herself stealing a peak at his rump which was perfectly round and full. As her eyes followed Dante's physique to the opposite end of the court, she noticed that he had been flagrantly fouled by someone on the blue team and that the referee didn't call it.

"Foul!" Celeste yelled jumping up. "He hacked him. What, are you blind?" Everyone in that section joined in her boycott. Dante looked up at her in the stands, shrugged his shoulders, then smiled. He gave her a "way to go" thumbs up. The referee glanced up at her too wondering who the heck she was to be calling him out like that. Realizing that she had made a scene she quickly took her seat. Jason clapped his hands and said to her, "Way to go Ms. Celeste."

By half time, the game was tied and the gym filled with more spectators. The second half was much more exciting with the blue team leading by two points with only fourteen seconds left on the clock. The inbound pass went to Dante, who shook, rattled and rolled the ball up the court. Faking and shaking with his head and body, Dante shook loose his opponent and went up for a three pointer with just two seconds left on the clock. SWISH! Nothing but net as the ball threaded the net for the game winner. Dante's teammates swarmed him like bees to honey, hugging and patting him all at once. The majority of the people in the gym were standing, clapping and chanting. The scene was chaotic yet exhilarating all at once.

Celeste sat in her seat waiting for some of the crowd to clear out before she starting walking down to where Dante was sitting. The guys were still congratulating Dante while he changed his tee-shirt. His eyes roamed the area until he spotted Celeste. He waved for her to come down and meet him.

"Hey star," she said placing a hand on his shoulder while he bent over to tie his sneakers.

"They almost got us, babe. But not to worry cause Sir Dante was here," he said confidently.

"A little sure of ourselves, aren't we?" she teased.

"Got to be babe. If not me, who? If not after a game thriller like this, when?"

They both laughed softly. It didn't bother her that Dante sounded a little cocky about his game because he had every right to be. After all, if it had not been for his shot, they would have lost the game. She admired the way he stood tall and felt comfortable about his talent and gift for the game. Why shouldn't he, she thought to herself. It was no different than the confidence she had in herself when working on one of her patients.

"What time is it?" Dante asked.

"Nine pm," Celeste replied.

"Well, I'm starving. What about you? Are you hungry?"

"Not really, but I'm sure I have something at my house. You're welcome to dinner, if you like."

"That sounds good, Celeste. Maybe I will take you up on your offer. But first I'll grab a fast shower," he said scooping her hand up with his. "You sure it's not too late?"

"I'm sure," she said clutching onto his hand.

"Where are you parked?"

"Over there," she said pointing to her car parked across the street. Dante walked her to the car and waited for her to start the engine before closing the door behind her.

"I'll follow you. Give me a second to pull around front okay?" Celeste nodded in the affirmative then watched Dante's long strides as he ran back across the street. She didn't want to get too close to this brother if she could help it. Especially since she just got out of the rut with Alvin. This new thing was going to be a challenge no doubt. She closed her eyes and rolled her head around her shoulders before seeing the flashing high beams behind her. Basically, she would have to be careful not to let Dante Lattimore bounce into her life with such fury only to possibly be ejected before they had a chance to finish the game.

"Lord help me out here. A girl can only take so much," she pleaded aloud merging into the street.

Four

Two months later . . .

For the last several weeks, Celeste found herself floating about her life like a space shuttle astronaut on the way to the moon. Nothing appeared to be too difficult to accomplish. No exam seemed too complex and no patient was too much to deal with. She had Dante to thank for her new and improved outlook on life. It had been ten weeks since she moved out from Alvin's quaint little apartment to discover the comforts of her own Shangri-La.

Things were progressing nicely with Dante's new friendship, she thought as she drove home. They were spending more and more time together: taking long walks in the park, cruising to Delaware, competitive games of chess and collectively putting together meals in each other's kitchen. After many discussions, sometimes at the most inopportune times, they came to the agreement that they would develop a firm friendship before slipping into anything physical. Dante's schedule was beginning to become more compact with basketball season rapidly approaching. He told Celeste that now was the time for him to develop his "game face" to prepare his players for the upcoming season.

NaNe was pleased with Celeste's new gentleman friend. One Sunday afternoon, after church, NaNe cooked one of her exquisite meals for Dante and Celeste. At NaNe's first glance, Celeste sensed that she was impressed. Who wouldn't be in awe of Dante's handsome build and GQ attire?

After the introductions, NaNe welcomed Dante into her home the same way she had welcomed so many guests. Giving him a quick once over, she embraced him with one of her wholesome hugs.

"It's good to meet you Dante," NaNe said smiling then directing them into the living room. "Celeste has told me many good things about you. Come on in and make yourself comfortable."

Dante followed Celeste into the living room, while NaNe went into the kitchen to put the finishing touch on her meal. Dante's nose filtered through the aroma and detected that the evening meal was a combination of collard greens, sweet potato pie, dinner rolls and a baked ham. A few minutes had passed before NaNe summoned Celeste and Dante to the kitchen.

NaNe sat across from Dante so that she could get a better view of him. After observing

him for a few minutes, she decided that he
had good home training. She liked the way
Dante handled himself at the dinner table. He
didn't shovel food into his mouth and he kept
his elbows off the table. NaNe caught Dante
staring at Celeste on more than one occasion
and realized that he was certainly smitten with
her granddaughter.

"Pass me the butter, sugar," NaNe said
looking at Celeste then at Dante before continuing. "Celeste tells me that you coach college basketball. What do you do in the off
season?" NaNe asked.

The question caught Dante by surprise. He
was prepared to discuss his coaching job, the
players, even his family upbringing. But to explain what he does during the off season?
There were some things he wasn't ready to
confess to Celeste yet, and he most certainly
wouldn't do it over a dinner table. Dante took
a moment and gathered his thoughts before
responding, "I do some private consulting."

"Oh yeah? What kind of consulting?" NaNe
questioned looking him directly in the eyes.

Celeste could tell Dante was uncomfortable
with NaNe's forwardness and thought it best
to intervene. "NaNe did you know that
Dante's mom is a teacher too?"

"Is that so?" NaNe said eyeing Dante. She
didn't like the way Celeste had diverted the
conversation away from the topic. And she really didn't care for the way Dante chose to take
the easy road out by not answering her ques-

tion. Uncharacteristically, NaNe relaxed and let her question drop.

"What's your mother's name?"

"Lydia Lattimore," Dante smiled. "She's been a teacher for twenty years."

"The name sounds vaguely familiar. It's been awhile for me. I've been retired for ten years now, you know? Those kids finally ran me out of there," NaNe laughed. Dante and Celeste joined in with the tension-breaking laughter.

The dinner conversation remained light yet informative for NaNe as she learned more about Dante's character and moral make-up. The icing on the cake came when Dante escorted Celeste and NaNe to the Adams Point section of Washington for some dessert and coffee. Although NaNe's feelings about Dante were transparent to Celeste, she still managed to pull Celeste to the side and caution her to take it slow.

Realizing that she had spent the last few minutes reminiscing about Dante and their meeting with NaNe, Celeste finally let out the deep breath she had been holding in. Her grandmother's approval was very important to her and she was happy that NaNe seemed impressed.

Backing into her parking space, she surveyed the parking lot for Dante's Black 300ZX, a developing habit she most definitely had to sever. Naturally, the 300ZX was nowhere to be found. She stepped out of the car, and walked towards her apartment. Once inside, she turned on the air conditioner, opened the blinds and grabbed the cordless phone to check her messages. She had traded in a day of studying at the library for a day of pampering. Looking at her newly polished toenails and fingernails, she was sure she had made the smart choice.

There were three messages on her voice mail. One from NaNe reminding her that it was the third Sunday in August and the church members would love to see her precious face in a pew tomorrow; one from Dante hinting if she could roll out of bed in enough time to attend service. The last message was from Alvin. This was Alvin's third message this week.

A few weeks back, Alvin had spotted her and Dante at the Summer Jazz festival. Dante had just left Celeste to go find a spot for them to set up the lawn chairs when Alvin walked up behind her.

"Well, I see you didn't waste too much time finding you a new man," Alvin said while giving her a level gaze.

"Excuse me?" Celeste replied, startled to see him.

"You heard me. Where's old lover boy going? Don't tell me you ran him away already with all your nagging and practical ways?"

"Leave me alone, Alvin," Celeste said, walking away.

"Was he the reason why you left?" he shouted.

"What?" Celeste gasped and stopped in her tracks. "I don't believe you're asking me that. Leave me alone. It's been two months since we broke up. What I do is none of your business anymore." She stormed off to find Dante.

Celeste was astounded by Alvin's words. He seemed out of control— crazy. Thank God she had managed to pull herself together before Dante returned to take her to their seats. Although, she wanted desperately to share with Dante her run in with Alvin, she chose to wait until a few days after the festival before telling him. Dante was furious that she had waited days after the festival to tell him about her confrontation with Alvin. But Celeste knew that had she told Dante about her and Alvin's escapade while at the festival, Dante would have hunted him down.

Since the scene at the jazz festival Alvin's calls hadn't stopped. In the beginning when the calls started, Celeste was flattered at the thought that it appeared Alvin was jealous. Then, after the fourth call in a thirty hour period, Celeste sensed that Alvin was more obsessed with her new relationship than winning her back.

Alvin could be cool, cold, or callous, but he was never frightening. To Celeste, Alvin had changed for the worse since they broke up. She wondered if he loved her more than he admitted. But no, Celeste reasoned, he would romance her back, rather than threaten her. Celeste was sure something crazy was happening in his life but she had no intentions of finding out. She simply wanted nothing to do with him.

All week he had harassed her at home with messages that he had to speak to her. Today was no different. He swore in his message that he needed to see her about something because his life could be in danger. "I'm in some business with Tony." She pressed the pound key on the phone and erased the message. Her safest bet was to avoid Alvin and his raving fits.

Deciding that her day of pampering was over, Celeste placed her slender oval-shaped reading glasses on and picked up her pharmacology book. She would have to start reviewing her notes now before her finals, which were scheduled three weeks away. Coming into this summer semester, she had managed to preserve a 3.6 grade point average. Her goal was to bring that up to a 4.0 by the time graduation came around next May so she could capture the summa-cum-laude award. What a great honor that would be for her and for her family to see her walking across the stage as the class president to receive the award. Celeste was determined to be the best and brightest dental student at Howard University.

Reflecting back on her standoff with Uncle Deak and even NaNe to a certain degree, she was happy that she stood up and fought for her right to do her own thing. People would often misunderstand her connection with NaNe. Her accusers, including Alvin, would refer to her as being weak, and easily persuaded by her grandmother's strong influence. The only thing Celeste was guilty of was respect. She truly admired and respected NaNe and her words of wisdom. No matter how many times NaNe got under her skin, Celeste managed to find a way to dismiss NaNe in a cordial way, while still standing firmly on her own decisions. After she got accepted to dental school and gave her two weeks notice to her government job, everyone knew that as silent as she had been about voicing her opinion, Celeste Dunbar was going to do what she felt was right for her and nobody else.

Although spending another four years in a classroom to specialize in surgery was not likely, Celeste had a back-up plan. Her other option, the one she'd most likely accept, was to do a one year internship at Johns Hopkins University Hospital and then find an area to start her practice. Of course, if NaNe had her choice, she would open a practice for Celeste in Washington the day after graduation so that Celeste could be forever cemented to the metropolis. Actually, Celeste wasn't all that thrilled about staying in the nation's capital, until she bumped into Dante Lattimore. Dante had cruised into her life with a certain kind of ease and focus similar to an experienced stick-shift driver. He didn't have to fumble around with the gearbox or her emotional needs. Strangely enough, Dante knew exactly how to handle Celeste. Unlike Alvin, Dante afforded Celeste the opportunity to feel very independent and appreciated. He always appeared genuinely interested in her feelings and opinions. Furthermore, Dante wasn't all that concerned about being right either. On the other side of the coin, Alvin always had to be in control and feel like the complete authority figure in their relationship. Whenever it came time for Celeste and Alvin to have a discussion about anything of grave significance, he always changed the situation to his advantage. Also Alvin had to have the last word. He was spoiled like that. Celeste figured it had to do with the issue of being tossed around from home to home trying to fit in wherever and whenever necessary. As a result of his inconsistent living arrangements, Alvin had developed a need to be heard, to be right, to be respected, to be rich, no matter what the cost.

Celeste didn't want to think about Alvin or his self-serving, materialistic wants and desires. The only thing that concerned her about Alvin and his recent antics was the seriousness in his voice. She knew that he was involved in some kind of business opportunity with Tony and that worried her. Celeste never felt comfortable with Tony and Alvin's friendship. Tony had an overpowering effect on Alvin, causing him to drop whatever he was doing anytime he called. After a while, Celeste gave up on trying to make Alvin see the light about the power Tony had over him since Alvin would defend Tony to the end and it would just cause more frustration and problems within their relationship.

The truth was unmistakable. Celeste detested Tony. Celeste felt that Tony was a bad influence on Alvin and knew how to manipulate him. What she didn't understand was why Tony was Alvin's best friend.

As time moved on, Celeste realized just how money-hungry he and Alvin both were. Tony would often make jokes about her living off Alvin's hard earned dollars while they had to bust their butts while they were in school. A statement Celeste knew was a blatant lie. She knew all about Uncle Franchesco and his bullying tactics that provided Alvin and Tony an opportunity to sail through Georgetown with the Gumichi wind behind them. Not detracting anything from their hard earned engineering accomplishments, Celeste refused to suck up to Tony and Alvin's self-proclaimed stardom.

She was sure whatever was going on with Alvin had everything to do with Tony Lucero and his big boss Uncle Franchesco. All Celeste had the strength to do for now, besides reading over her lesson, was to say a silent prayer for Alvin and his well-being. For some heart-wrenching reason, she could feel that Alvin was in need of a few more guardian angels. She only hoped and prayed her intuition would be wrong.

* * *

Dante greeted the other coaches in the room excusing himself along the way. He located his best buddy, Coach Johnson, a rebelling coach out of Indianapolis, on the opposite side of the room. He acknowledged CJ and pointed to the door. The traditional thing to do after the Coalition meeting was to grab a couple of coaches and head over to a neighborhood grill for a few beers.

He hadn't seen CJ since last season when they met during the playoffs to settle who had the best team. Of course, CJ and his Colt following, Pacer applauding, Bobby Knight worshipping players, beat his team in overtime 100 to 99. Dante was heartbroken and downright pissed with his players for losing that game. Mainly because it was so important to him to personally shut CJ and his forever Notre Dame praising, Purdue hooting, mouth. Dante let out a devious smile as he greeted CJ with a coach's hug and back pat. "Yo man what's up you low-life . . ."

"Coach D," CJ said grinning widely. "Don't tell me you're still sore about last year," CJ said waving his hand. "Man, you need to let that go. Matter of fact you need to prepare your players for another whupping this year." Both men chuckled lightly in anticipation that they probably would meet again on the courts for the championship this year.

CJ was a little shorter and somewhat stockier than Dante. But that didn't stop CJ from fussing and cussing, screaming and yelling, pointing and kicking at anyone, no matter what size his opponents were. CJ was a fierce, intense, sometimes fanatical, competitor. This was cool with Dante because they were both cut from the same cloth, athletically speaking. Dante was a star track runner and football player, and CJ a star basketball guard and strong baseball pitcher. The two had met in college and maintained a healthy friendship over the ten year span since graduation. Dante was the best man in CJ's wedding and the godfather of his son, Jamaal.

Examining his buddy's profile for a moment, CJ blurted, "What's her name?"

"What are you talking about?"

"Don't play me, Dante. I know when you've got babe-itis. I can see it in your stance."

"What kind of bull is that? If you can't make any better observations than that you need to retire," Dante teased, shaking his head in a hopeless type gesture.

"What's the young lady's name?"

"Celeste Dunbar," Dante found himself saying shyly.

CJ studied his friend's body language for a moment longer in an attempt to pick up more information. Since he began his career in coaching, CJ had become a master at interpreting body language. His friend's movements told him that Dante respected Celeste. Truthfully, he was happy for his best friend. Dante was long overdue for something vivacious in his life.

"Let's order something to eat and you can tell me all about her."

Dante took a break to catch his breath, after summarizing his meeting with Celeste, providing an opportunity for CJ to fire up some more questions.

"Is this just a passing fling or are you thinking of taking her home to Mother?" CJ said leaning over the table toward Dante.

"I don't think it's a fling. At least on my part. Now about taking her home to meet Moms, we'll have to wait and see on that one. Time will tell. She invited me to go with her to her family reunion in North Carolina next weekend," Dante said, stuffing two french fries in his mouth.

"Oh really?" CJ replied raising his left eyebrow. "Pass the ketchup man." The two were quiet for a few seconds while CJ slapped the bottom of the ketchup bottle and Dante took a bite out of his double cheeseburger.

"Are you going?" CJ asked, after sipping some of his beer.

"I suppose so," Dante replied. "I don't have any other plans. I still have a few more weeks to strategize on how we're going to whoop your butt during the finals." Dante was laughing now.

"In your dreams, brother," CJ chuckled along. "So, you two been intimate yet?"

Dante frowned slightly at CJ's inappropriate question. CJ could sense Dante's discomfort but didn't back down from the question. If this girl meant that much to his friend, he had to know how she was treating him.

"Not yet."

"Good. Hold out for as long as you can. This way you won't be confused about her sincerity. Besides, it'll build character and stamina," CJ laughed.

"And I suppose you're speaking from experience? Please! I'm sure you didn't waste any time testing your stamina out with Monica. So, don't give me that builds stamina, yak, yak, yak."

They sat and talked for a few more hours before ending their evening. Dante promised CJ to bring Celeste to their game for good luck if they met in the finals. CJ left saying if she was going to be the reason for their win then he could very well wait until the holidays to meet her.

Driving home, Dante was relieved to have shared some insight with his friend about Celeste and his feelings for her. It had been a while since he had met a woman who was able to stimulate his mind the way Celeste had done. Initially, he admitted to himself, the initial attraction toward Celeste was physical. But after spending a few hours with her at the tiny cafe, Dante knew that Celeste's beauty was only part of the reason why he was captivated by her.

After several, unsteady relationships, mostly due to Dante's heavy schedule, he had vowed to himself that his name and love didn't be-

long in the same sentence. However, Celeste
had placed a crack right down the middle of
that theory. She was unique from any of the
women he'd ever dated. Her personality was
filled with spontaneity, humor and honesty.
She exuded a strong sense of self while maintaining her softness and radiant sensuality.
Her humble nature and genuine concern for
the well being of others made her all the more
appealing. Dante smiled as he pulled into the
parking lot and noticed the pony car parked.
Never before had he even considered anyone
as a possible wife. Until Celeste.

Five

"Are you nervous?" Celeste asked, glancing over at Dante. The convertible top was down and the wind blowing across her face. She felt as though there was nothing more invigorating than sucking in a breath of fresh air on a long journey. Luckily, her hair was protected from the wind under a fitted straw hat.

"Not particularly," he responded leaning his head against the headrest. "I've attended several family reunions. They're all about the same. Don't you think?"

Celeste laughed to herself. That might apply to his family but the Dunbar clan was another story. "Perhaps," she said holding his hand while keeping her left hand on the steering wheel. She yawned and then shook her head a few times in an attempt to fight off the sleepy feeling.

She was exhausted after staying up late all this week studying for her exams. She was sure that she did well on all her exams. But you never know about the professors, she thought. When NaNe called last week to remind her about the family reunion, she didn't feel all that much like attending. Now that her finals were over and she had a few weeks to regroup, she felt the excitement about the Dunbar event overwhelming her.

Dante had agreed to make the seven-hour drive to North Carolina with her, and she was happy to have him seated next to her. Looking over at him once more, her heart began racing. She was happy, elated that Dante had come into her life.

"Dante," she smiled turning her head slightly toward him. "Would you like to drive Beauty?"

Dante straightened up in his seat, leaned against the car door on an angle to get a fuller glimpse of Celeste and said surprisingly, "You'd let me sit behind the wheel?"

She gave him a quick glare, turned up her top lip slightly and replied, "Of course!" Cautiously, she made her way across the highway over onto the shoulder. Once the car was at a complete stop, Celeste unfastened her seat belt and then turned her body to face Dante. "So, you want to drive her?"

Dante grabbed Celeste's hand and whispered, "I'd rather do something else. But I guess this will do."

Celeste walked around to the back of the car, playfully brushing up against Dante. "How about a kiss, loverboy?" she said wrapping her slender arms around his neck. Dante obliged, although he knew he would have to fight hard to keep his nature from awakening.

"There. That's better," she whispered heading over to the passenger side of the car. Trucks were passing at an enormous speed causing the car to rock. "Be careful, Dante," Celeste warned as he made his way around to the driver's side.

Once in the driver's seat, Dante adjusted his seat, the rearview mirror and buckled his seat belt. Bending over toward Celeste, he placed a wet kiss on her lips. He wiggled in the seat a little and put the car in gear. "Hold on, Beauty," he said tapping the dashboard. "Daddy's in the driver's seat now."

Alvin took a deep puff of the home made cigarette dangling from his lips. Pacing back and forth on the carpet barefoot, he slowly exhaled the smoke through his nostrils. The telephone had been ringing out of control for the last few hours so he decided to take it off the hook. *How did he get in this mess?* He frowned exhaling more smoke. He had left Celeste a slew of messages over the past few weeks in the hopes of her returning the calls. Not even his urgent messages elicited a response from his ex-love.

He sank down into the sofa and picked up the bottle of beer. Empty! "Damn," he shouted walking toward the kitchen area. He knew something vile was going on with Franchesco Gumichi and his entourage. He was totally in the dark since Tony fell out of contact with him over the past few weeks. Even the unfamiliar voices on his answering machine threatening his life about some stolen money was confusing. What was going on? Opening his fifth bottle of beer, Alvin hurriedly tilted the bottle back and gulped down the liquid. He stopped abruptly when he heard the pounding on his front door.

Like a fox sneaking up on its prey, Alvin tiptoed over to the door and looked out the peep hole. Standing on the opposite side of the wooden door were two muscular men somewhat overdressed for this time of year. Alvin backed away from the door with the same kind of lightness as he had approached it. Running past the dining room, he snatched his wallet off the table and his shirt off the back of the chair. He had to make it to the bedroom window before the men broke the door down.

The heavy knocking was more demanding now. No sooner than he closed the bedroom door behind him, he heard the front door cave in. Pausing briefly, Alvin glared at the bedroom door, heart racing wildly. *What the hell do they want?* he wondered silently. The sounds of dishes crashing and things being broken snapped him back to the present state of emergency. He had to make it to that window before they made it through the bedroom door. Leaping over the bed in one jump, Alvin lifted the window and put one foot over the ledge. The bedroom door swung open savagely as one of the men ran over to the window. "Hey!" he yelled reaching out for Alvin.

Alvin, barely missing the man's grasp, swung his other leg over the ledge, jumped down and landed in the shrubbery below him. "Good thing Celeste talked me into the first floor apartment," he exhaled springing from the bushes. It wasn't until he ran onto the hot, rough concrete that he noticed he was still barefoot. Once he got further from the apartment, he ducked behind a building and buttoned his shirt. Glaring around the building, he spotted a pay phone across the street. Crossing the street quickly, he slipped into the half booth. Holding the phone between his chin and shoulder, Alvin's eyes roamed the area for the familiar but not so friendly faces. After three rings, the voice on the other end picked up.

"Trevor? Is that you man?"

"Yeah. Alvin?"

"Man listen. I've only got a second to talk. Something's going down with me and I need some time to figure things out. All I know is that I'm barefoot and out of breath," he said breathing hard. "Can I swing by there?"

"Naw mon. Things hot around ere too. Some European boys been in ere lookin for ya. Meet me at my crib in tirty minutes," he sang in his thick Jamaican accent.

Alvin hung up the phone with a blank expression on his face. Unconsciously, he waved down a taxi. "Southwest side," he told the driver in a catatonic sound as he slid into the back seat.

Why were those guys so angry? he wondered. He knew who probably sent them. The only thing he did was help Tony devise a computer program that would allow Uncle Franchesco to penetrate the federal government and its witness protection program via modem access to the fed's computer files with the informational disks Gumichi had given him. And since Alvin had occasional access, as a top, independent computer contractor, to the federal files, he was just the man to make the job complete. He had done everything according to plan so far. He created the program and interlinked it with the fed's computer system and copied it onto some disks. He was in the final stages when Tony called him two weeks ago frantic about reaching the deadline for Uncle Franchesco. Alvin figured Tony was exaggerating slightly because he was anxious to get the money from his uncle. One hundred fifty thousand dollars would be their reward for pulling the job off. But, there was a catch to it as usual. They had to make a quick stop somewhere and make a business transaction for Gumichi. Something Tony had neglected to mention to him when he first approached him about this so-called business opportunity. Now it had been two weeks since the mix-up and since he last saw Tony, who promised to handle everything with his uncle. Damn! Alvin huffed. He didn't want to think about that night anymore if he could help it.

As far as Alvin could figure, everything was going along just fine. The only thing notice-

ably different in the last two weeks was the fact
that he hadn't heard from Tony. Then it hit
him like a boxer being sucker punched unexpectedly. Tony must be at the bottom of this
mess somehow. Who else would know to look
for him at the frequented reggae joint? Tony
had sold him out, he frowned falling back
against the taxi seat from exhaustion. "That
son of a . . . ." he cursed under his breath. "He
set me up. But how? Why?"

Six

"Little Bit!" yelled Uncle Deak walking over to Celeste with arms open wide.

"Uncle Deak," she sang playfully giving him a hug. "You look distinguished as always." She was referring to his salt and pepper hair, mustache and beard. Uncle Deak resembled Ben, the minister on the popular 700 Club Christian Broadcast station. "This is my friend Dante," she said gingerly pulling Dante forward by the arm.

Uncle Deak scanned Dante's body up and down then extended his right hand, "Welcome to the Dunbar family reunion. Good to meet you."

"Same here," Dante smiled returning the handshake.

"Ya'll come on in and make yourself welcomed."

Uncle Deak took great pleasure in introducing Dante around to the family members while giving him a quick tour of the property. He had done a fabulous job with his six bedroom, four bathroom, architecturally designed home, Dante thought, absorbing the picturesque view.

The house sat on ten acres of plush, green land enclosed by a picket fence. In the back of the house, flowing through a majority of the land, was a freshwater stream that led to a small pond. There was a small bridge built to cross the stream to get to the far side of the property which had a gazebo and a few picnic tables.

Several pine, apple, eucalyptus, and oak trees, along with a number of different plant life and various plant and rock formations, landscaped the property throughout. On the front side of the house, off the family room, was a red wood deck that Uncle Deak finished himself. The house had so many wonderful attributes that it was hard to believe that Uncle Deak resided here alone. He'd never remarried after his wife, Lucille, died some ten years ago. Since that time, Deak Dunbar was content and quite happy living as a single man.

He had one child, Iris, who spent most of her time in Europe as a runway model for a top modeling agency. Although Uncle Deak protested viciously about Iris' decision to sow her oats abroad, she being a little like Celeste, ignored his ranting fits and boarded the plane departing for London anyway. Uncle Deak smiled while he studied Celeste, as she walked arm in arm with Dante across the yard. Celeste and Iris, first cousins with similar habits yet different views, were inseparable as children. However, with all the traveling Iris did, it had been hard for Celeste and Iris to spend as much time together. But they always managed to call or write once a month to keep each other motivated. After five years, Uncle Deak managed to deal with seeing his baby girl a couple of times a year. Besides, whenever they got too lonely for each other, someone dropped a plane ticket in the mail.

There were at least seventy relatives and close friends scattered about the Dunbar estate enjoying Uncle Deak's barbecue and wide-open space. The younger Dunbar children were involved in a variety of games and activities, ranging from volleyball and croquet to double Dutch and dominos. Naturally, a soulful family reunion would not be complete without the O'Jays *family reunion* song blaring out of the speakers and the Don Correlius & the Soul Train family dance line. Aunt Mackie, a pretty brown-skinned woman with freckles and a good size pair of hips, started the Soul Train line as she slid on down the line, swinging those hips to the Sounds Of Blackness' *I Believe*. The younger children egged her on singing, "Go Aunt Mackie." Uncle Eddie met her midway down the line trying to do his best rendition of the butterfly dance. The children laughed at Uncle Eddie's poor attempt of trying to weave his knees in and out. Uncle Deak followed behind them bopping and spinning down the line, while Dante grabbed Celeste's hand and led her down the line with the fierce sounds of the choir still bellowing. Before long, the line had dismantled with everyone jamming to the music with their own best dance steps. Even Al Green's *Love & Happiness* didn't keep the younger generation from finger popping to his soulful crooning.

The atmosphere at the Dunbar family reunion was filled with euphoria. There was so much love and unity exuding from every person. The unification was solid and everyone opted to have a wonderful time at this annual, traditional family gathering. Everyone was proud to be a part of history as the raid of bright orange tee-shirts, listing the family tree, served as the choice of apparel for the day.

Dante fell right in sync with the Dunbar members, particularly the children. They invited him to participate in all the games from softball to jumping rope. Asia, Celeste's youngest cousin became infatuated with Dante.

"Come on Dante," Asia said pulling him by the hand. "We want you to be on our team." Asia was Aunt Mackie's granddaughter.

Dante grinned, knelt down beside the little girl and said, "Dante needs to take a little break. How about I come back in a little while and we can play then?"

"Why not now?" the little girl whined.

"Cause I'm much older than you and I need to get more break time than you guys," he smiled.

"You're old? Wow, you're old like my mommie and daddy, huh?" she said patting his hand. "It's okay. Go ahead and take your nap, then you can come play with us later." Dante laughed as the little girl ran away yelling to the rest of the children that Dante had to go take his nap.

Celeste tiptoed up behind him and poked him in the side. He jumped slightly then turned around and said, "Hey gorgeous where you been?"

"Making my rounds. Looks like you found a new friend. Asia seems really attached to you."

"She's so cute. How old is she?"

"Four."

"Four?" Dante said raising an eyebrow. "That's all? She's bright. It's got to be a Dunbar trait."

"Flattery will get you places here, bro," she taunted.

"Truly?" he said drawing her near and placing a kiss on her lips. "What else do I need to say baby?"

"Come on boy," she snickered pulling away. "We're about to have the family history read to us. As if I don't know it by heart now." Dante followed behind her thinking about her little cousin Asia who had captured his heart. Perhaps he would settle down soon and have a child of his own. With any luck, maybe he and Celeste could build something solid that would lead to having their own family reunion one day.

The sun was beginning to cast its orange rays over the Dunbar clan as it slid its way down below the mountains. Earlier in the day, when they had approached the large, sunny, kitchen, Aunt Ruthie, Aunt Mackie, Cousin Charlotte, NaNe, Cousin Lena and Mother Williams were all strategically situated. It was as if they were planning to ambush Dante and Celeste. And that is exactly what they did.

Celeste clinched onto Dante's arm as she led him through the veteran female Dunbar clan. "We were beginning to think you forgotten all about us suga," Aunt Mackie frowned, hugging Celeste.

"Everyone, this is Dante," Celeste said confidently still holding his arm. "Dante, this is the Dunbar arsenal." Dante broke free from Celeste's embrace. Making his way around to each matriarch, he showered them with hugs as he officially introduced himself. Saving the best for last, he gave NaNe a bear hug.

"Well now, Dante," Cousin Charlotte chimed in looking at Dante from head to toe over her tiny spectacles. "We hear that you're a college coach in Washington. Is that so?"

"Yes ma'am," Dante responded sitting upright in his chair. "I coach basketball."

"Is that a stable living? I mean does it have some future in it? What do you do in the off season?" Cousin Lena questioned, moving closer to Dante.

"I do some private consulting," he replied dryly.

"Really? Just what kind of consulting?" Cousin Lena continued with her quizzing.

"I guess you could say I do some private consulting of sorts," he replied dryly. Celeste flinched a little bit when she heard Dante's reply. It was the same answer he gave NaNe several weeks ago. She would have to find out exactly what kind of consulting he did during his off season. In fact, as soon as she got the chance, she was going to address this well dodged question.

"Did I hear you graduated from college in the midwest? What did you get your degree in?" Aunt Ruthie butted in.

The questions were flying faster than a 20 second time out. He could feel his head starting to swarm and silently prayed that the Q&A period would come to an end sooner than later. Before long, Mother Williams, the eldest matriarch and Queen Bee of the clan, rose up from her chair with her wooden cane and tapped it on the granite kitchen floor till she had everyone's attention. Keeping her steady hum under her breath, she peered over at Dante. "Everyone hush!" she warned waving her cane. You're scaring him half to death. Come on over here to Mother Williams, Dante," she said waving her hand toward him. "Come on here, I ain't gonna bite you."

Dante rose to his feet and strolled over to the other side of the kitchen, near the bay window, where Mother Williams had been sitting for the last thirty minutes. He stood towering over her with a perplexed look. "Yes ma'am?"

"Sit down, son," she instructed tapping her cane on the empty oak rocker. After Dante took his seat, she sat down across from him.

Everyone in the kitchen was silent, waiting to hear what Mother Williams had to say. Everyone, including Celeste, was focused on Mother Williams and Dante.

Mother Williams stared at Dante a little while longer, still humming loud enough for only her ears to hear. Then, she cleared her throat and with the lightest, sweetest, voice one could imagine, said, "Dante, how you truly feel about all these women throwing the damnedest questions at you?"

Dante let out a light laugh and said, "Honestly, Mother Williams, I feel somewhat overwhelmed. Only because I just met everyone for the first time a few minutes ago."

"And I suppose if you had to do it all over again, you'd stayed outside there with the men, huh?"

Dante smiled, looked down at his feet for a second contemplating his answer. Mother Williams was absolutely right. If he had to do it over, he would be outside with the Dunbar men standing over the barbecue grill, sipping on a beer, instead of being grilled himself. Raising both his eyebrows, he brought his eyes level with Mother Williams' eyes, "Yes ma'am."

Mother Williams laughed loudly along with everyone else in the kitchen. "Then," she said placing her cane down on the floor then leaning on it to get up out of the chair, "I suggest you go on out there with the men and leave these noisy women in here to tend to their own business."

Dante leaped up, glanced around at the faces staring at him in the kitchen, kissed Mother Williams on the cheek and said, "Thanks, Mother Williams. I owe you one."

"Go on, get out of here," she laughed. Dante bolted out of the kitchen quicker than a groundhog popping its head out of its hole. Celeste got up to follow behind him but stopped when she heard Mother Williams say, "No, no missy, not you. You stay right here and let him breathe. I don't know why you feel it necessary to be all up under him any-how. It's not lady-like for nice girls to be traips-ing behind a man. Let him come to you, honey. You young women spend too much time chasing these men. It's like a bird's nest on the ground. The men ain't even got to work for nothing no more when it comes to dating."

Of course, Mother Williams was right as usual, Celeste thought sitting back down in her chair. After all, she had been around a lot longer than everyone in the kitchen. She was ninety years old and had a memory as good as any twenty one year old. Mother Williams had taught NaNe, Cousin Charlotte, Aunt Mackie and Aunt Ruthie the ropes of life when it came to men, marriage and money. When Mother Williams was younger, she spent many hours in the kitchen teaching her daughters, nieces and little cousins how to cook and clean house so they could "get and keep" good husbands. And, they all had hitched good men and had plenty of money in the bank, too.

Two or so hours had passed before the rap session in the kitchen ended. The mosquitoes managed to fight their way around the green-colored lights hanging on a string and incense smoke hovering in the air, to chase most everyone into the house. There were a few brave warriors who decided to wrestle with the pesky bugs. Dante was one of the brave soldiers. Celeste went outside to join Dante on the wooden swing. The moon was full and the stars twinkled throughout the sky. They really didn't need the little green lights strung throughout the back yard to see. The moon seemed brighter than normal and the cool breeze kept the windchimes singing in the background.

"I love it down here," Celeste said resting her head on Dante's shoulder. "It's so peaceful, so tranquil. I just love it. Especially nights like this."

"It's relaxing here, that's for certain. Perhaps I should think about buying some property down this way. Your uncle told me that the man up the street is selling pieces of his property at a good price. What ya think? Could you get used to this being our little hideaway?" he asked kissing her on the forehead.

"I most certainly could," she said standing. "You feel like taking a stroll?"

"Only if you promise not to take advantage

of me in the dark. I'm scared of the dark, you know?" he winked, whispering into her ear. "You'll protect me. Right baby?"

"Of course, I will sweetness. Trust me," she grinned seductively. "Give me your hand. I'll lead the way."

They walked hand in hand toward the back of the house until the string of green lights was invisible. The moonlight guided their path as they crossed the man made bridge to the other side of the stream. It was pitch black in the back of the house and very quiet, except for the crickets that echoed from time to time. Celeste led Dante into the gazebo where Uncle Deak had built a wide circular bench. The moonlight was bouncing off the oak panels as the night wind whistled the leaves on the large oak tree. Celeste motioned for Dante to take a seat on the bench as she stood in front of him wedged between his legs. "It's still pretty warm out here, don't you think?" Celeste said fanning her shirt.

"Perhaps we should take a dip in the stream," he said raising his brow.

"Is that right," she grinned sitting down in his lap.

"Yup," he nodded sucking her left cheek lightly.

"That tickles, Dante. Stop," she said giggling and trying to move her face away from his lips. After a few minutes of attempting to break free from Dante's grasp, Celeste finally gave in. She let him suck on her cheek a few seconds longer before bursting out with more laughter.

"You're so ticklish," he said poking her in her side.

Celeste was out of control now, laughing hysterically and moving away from him the best she could. Dante got such a kick out of seeing her laugh and squirm at the same time that he continued to pick at her until tears from too much laughter began running down her face.

"Stop it, Dante," she whined then let her body fall back against the bench. She could see the stars scattered about the sky as she lay back on the wood.

"Okay," he grinned. "I'll stop. Come here baby," he said motioning her to sit back down on his lap.

"No way," she replied sitting up. "I'm not going to fall for that line."

Dante put on his most sincere face. "I'm serious Celeste. I promise I won't tickle you anymore, today. Not unless I have to come over there and get you."

Celeste stood up and walked over to Dante then took her sat in his lap once more. *What tight thighs,* she thought silently. Gently, Dante took her face in his large hands and lightly turned it until it faced his. Celeste could feel her heart racing. She had dreamed about this for the last few months, ever since he'd tried to kiss her in the clinic. In fact, she was a little put off by the fact that it had taken him this long to try and fully kiss her. She had adopted the attitude that she wasn't going to try and kiss him unless he tried to kiss her first. And thank God, she smiled, she had waited.

Dante lightly pressed his soft lips onto Celeste's lips. He could feel his temperature rising as he fought to control his excitement. He could also feel his nature pushing its way up as he engulfed her tongue with his. The kiss lasted for several minutes before they both came up for air.

"I think I'm falling in love," Dante whispered drawing her near while laying down on the bench.

Celeste was lying directly on top of Dante and felt his hardness. *Just as she thought,* she assessed, quietly astonished by the curve his nature had taken. *The brother is well endowed.* Celeste rested her head in the palm of her hand. Staring at him for a few moments, she replied, "How do you know?"

"Because I've never been this excited or wanted to spend so much time with any woman before. You're like a drug, Celeste. I think about you whenever I can, and I think about you whenever I'm supposed to be thinking about something else."

"Yeah I know," she said kissing him on the nose. "The same thing happens to me. Sometimes when I'm in the clinic, I catch myself looking up at the door wishing you would walk through it. I guess we're both catching that contagious virus they call love, huh?"

"I guess so," he responded, pulling her head toward his then intertwining his tongue with hers again. For the first time, Dante's hands perused her body. Celeste felt Dante's hands glide up her shirt and across the bottom of her bare back. The kisses lingered while Dante's hands continued to explore Celeste's back.

"You're so soft," he moaned into her ear. Then he let his hands work their way around to the front part of her body. A few minutes later, Dante sprang up abruptly, startling Celeste.

"What's wrong?" she said sitting up with him.

"Nothing." He was standing now and motioning her to stand on her feet as well. "I think we should take that dip in the stream now," he said tugging her by the hand.

"The water is going to be cold Dante," Celeste said pulling him back down toward the bench.

"Yeah, well, I probably need to be splashed with something cold to cool me off," he said sitting beside her, then nibbling on her ear.

Carefully, Dante lay back on the bench, inching Celeste down toward him. Celeste fell on top of Dante crawling up his body until she was breath to breath with him.

"Celeste," Dante whispered running his fingers up her back.

"Yes, baby," she said positioning her lips closer to his lips.

"You're very special. You know that don't you?"

"Yes. And so are you," she said kissing him on his neck.

"Good. Because I want you to know that I'm in it for more than just this."

"Me too Dante."

"I'm glad to hear that sweetheart," he said tossing her hair. "And Celeste, take it easy on a brother," he smiled.

"Oh, I will," she grinned. "I'll take it nice and easy."

Seven

Alvin reached Trevor's house exactly thirty
minutes after he spoke to him. Racing up the
stairs two at a time, he reached the top of the
landing and banged on the front door.

"Come on in, Alvin," Trevor said pulling him
into the house quickly. "Man, you look like you
had a rough day. Let me get ya a beer ey?"

"That would be good Trevor. Thanks,"
Alvin said following Trevor down the narrow
hallway into the small kitchen.

"So, what is all the fuss going on with you
mon? I've got fat European boys casing my joint
for ya; I've got you standing here in me livin
room barefoot. Tell me what's going on little
bro?" Trevor said eyeing Alvin up and down.

"I don't know where to begin," Alvin exhaled taking a seat at the kitchen table.

"Well ya better start somewhere because
word on the street is you jerked Franchesco
Gumichi out of some serious cashflow."

Alvin stared out the tiny kitchen window for
a few minutes temporarily losing himself in
Trevor's garden. Ever since he met Trevor, he
always maintained a vegetable garden. Alvin's

eyes soared past the green tomatoes then landed on the patch of cabbage before Trevor's voice carried him back inside the house.

"Say mon, what ya doing? Did you swindle Gumichi out of his money?" Trevor could decipher from Alvin's facial expression that he had hurt his pride. But, he had to know just how much of a crater his friend had dug himself into.

"Trevor," Alvin said lowly as he stood up from the chair, "I had some time to think about this on the way over here and I know who's behind this mess." Alvin opened up the cabinet door beneath the kitchen sink and pulled out the trash can. Tossing the bottle in the trash, he tucked the plastic can back under the sink then washed his hands. "You have some sandals or sneakers I can slip on?"

Trevor glanced at Alvin then went into the hall closet and pulled out a pair of tan sandals. "Here," he said tossing the sandals at Alvin. "Now don't ask me for nothing else till ya tell me what the hell is going on."

"Tony and I worked up a program that could possibly allow Franchesco to infiltrate the FBI witness protection program. The program was damn near complete. After some tedious hacking, I was finally able to interface the FBI systems at work with the program we created. In fact, I copied them on some disks, tucked them in my gym bag and threw it in the locker at the gym. For some reason, I didn't feel comfortable bringing them home.

Call it a weird vibe or intuition but something told me not to bring them home. Anyway, Tony and I were supposed to meet Franchesco and give him the disks and pick up the money. I called Tony and told him I was ready. All he had to do was set up a time for the meeting. Actually, I figured we would just swing by his uncle's house and complete the transaction. That's all, I swear. I don't know why these guys are looking for me," Alvin lied. He knew why he was being chased. He hadn't spoken to Tony in two weeks. He hadn't returned his calls or tried to contact him. Something had gone deadly wrong.

Trevor studied his friend for a while before saying, "I don't understand mon. Why would you get involved in tis? Don't you know if you're busted, you'd be doing some big jail time? What yer tinking?"

"I wasn't thinking Trevor. All I know is that we had a chance to make some easy money if we did what Gumichi proposed us to do. The government hired me to create programs for special projects because they know I'm the best in the field. With the right information and enough time, I can bypass any system in my sleep. It's a gift. Besides, there's no way the government would be able to tie me into anything. Especially since I have clearance to work in the most top secret areas," Alvin said.

Pacing back and forth again, Alvin cursed under his breath then slammed the beer bottle on the counter.

"Easy mon, don't tear up my stuff. Why don't we try and figure this out before it gets too much more outta hand. I would hate to have to call the posse down here, you know? Chill. Everything work out no matter what ere? Main ting to do is to put dem disk somewhere safe. Somewhere they can't ever find em until you settle this matter with Franchesco. I'll put the word out on the street to find out what's up with Tony. Perhaps once we find him we'll make head or tail of the situation. Stay here for as long as you want. At least till things cool off. Don't want nothing happening to ya all right?"

"Thanks man," Alvin said slapping Trevor with the brotherly handshake. "The sooner this crap is solved the better off everybody will be. I still can't believe that punk Tony dogged me like that. And to think, I thought we were cool like brothers."

"Trust me Alvin mon. Ain't nobody like your brother but your brother and then sometimes that ain't even guaranteed."

Celeste backed into her parking space then shut the engine off. The trip to North Carolina had been a good idea after all, she thought looking over at Dante, who was staring out the window. Ever since they entered the DC perimeter, Celeste had tried to find out more about Dante's past.

Holding the keys in her hand, Celeste looked over at Dante and said, "Why don't you want to be more specific about what you do in the off season?"

"I told you, sweetheart, I am a consultant," he said opening the car door then stepping out.

"I know. You said that already. I was just curious as to what kind of consulting work you do. That's all."

"I solve problems for various types of businesses and agencies," he curtly responded. He really didn't want to talk about this subject anymore. "Why don't you go unlock the door? I'll grab the stuff and bring it in."

Celeste walked up the pathway to her apartment feeling frustrated by her inability to get a more specific answer out of Dante. Why was he so touchy about the subject? He didn't even want to discuss his previous relationships or anything of that nature. It was like he was deliberately trying to hide or avoid something. Perhaps he just needed more time to open up, she resolved. Celeste decided to let it drop for now but she was going to get more information about his past if it was the last thing she did.

Celeste stopped abruptly in her tracks when she noticed her front door cracked open. Dante was crunched over unloading their bags from the trunk of the car when Celeste tapped him on the shoulder. "Honey, somebody's been in my house."

"What?" Dante said turning around quickly. "What do you mean? Is the door open?"

"Yeah. And from what little bit I can see, it looks like they trashed my place too."

"Damn," Dante snapped, making his way up the small walk way before standing in front of Celeste's cracked door. "What the hell," he frowned poking his head in the doorway to get a closer inspection of her place. Books, albums, tapes, and pillows were scattered all over the living room. The plants and the sofa had been flipped over. "Seems like they weren't interested in your stereo or television or VCR." Backing away from the door, he grabbed her hand. "We'd better go over to my place and call the police."

To Dante it seemed as though Celeste's home had been searched. Plus, it seemed professional. He looked on as Celeste explained to the police officers how she had left the apartment and that she hadn't noticed anybody suspicious on the apartment grounds before her trip. Dante wondered if her innocent-looking face was hiding a dark secret.

Plopping down on Dante's sofa, Celeste dropped her face into her hands. She didn't understand what had happened and why it had happened to her. Dante eased next to her on the sofa, tossing the oversize pillows out of the way. "Here," he said motioning to her to take the cup. "It's hot, be careful."

"What is it?" she questioned inhaling the steam rising from the cup. "It smells good."

"It's chamomile tea with a squeeze of lemon. It will calm your nerves." Dante watched Celeste as she timidly sipped the tea. He wondered if she was hiding anything from him. And if so, why?

"Feeling better?" he asked.

"Considering? Yes."

"Good. Lay back and relax for a minute," he uttered, tugging her gently.

Celeste fell back into Dante's arms and chest as he leaned back against the sofa.

"Listen sweetheart," Dante said, "there's nothing else we can do tonight. Thankfully the maintenance technican will fix the locks tonight. Tell me Celeste, do you have any idea who might have done this?"

Celeste held her breath for a minute, then slowly exhaled, "Maybe. I don't know. Perhaps it's purely coincidental."

"Why do you say that? Do you know who it is?"

Celeste caressed Dante's right hand lightly while cupping the warm mug in her left hand. Clearing her throat she mumbled, "I didn't think about it until now. I think it could have something to do with Alvin and his dealings with Tony Lucero and his uncle Franchesco Gumichi."

Dante sat up abruptly nearly causing Celeste to spill the hot liquid. "Franchesco Gumichi?" he frowned. "You mean the mobster?"

"Yeah. That's the one."

"Why would Alvin associate with Gumichi? And why would he jeopardize your safety?"

"I don't know, Dante," she shrugged. "Alvin and Tony have been friends forever. Personally,

I always thought Tony was a bad influence on Alvin. But Alvin feels a sense of loyalty to Tony since Gumichi got him and Tony into George-town."

"Is that right?" Dante muttered raising his left eyebrow. "But why do you think they came to your place? Did you tell Alvin where you moved?"

"No. But he has my phone number and it's easy enough to get my address from the phone book. Maybe Gumichi was the reason Alvin began leaving such puzzling messages."

"Did he say he felt threatened?"

Celeste paused for a minute taking time to reflect on Alvin's past messages. "No, but I know that he and Tony were working on some project or business deal with the Gumichis."

Dante felt his palms itch. "Really? What kind of project? Did he elaborate?"

"Nope. Alvin had a habit of saying only enough to keep you plugged in and that's all."

"What does Alvin do?" he asked, his suspi-cions rising.

"He works as some hot shot independent programmer for various government agencies. Hey," she said turning to face Dante. "What's with all the questions? What, you writing a book or something?" she teased.

Alvin jumped up when he heard the front door lock click. He had dozed off and lost track of his whereabouts. Trevor walked through the living room archway just as Alvin was dodging behind the sofa.

"Relax mon. It's only me," Trevor smiled tossing the grocery bags on the coffee table.

"Whew!" Alvin uttered taking a deep breath then releasing it. "I thought it could have been your boys coming back for me."

"Them comin over ere? I tink not mon. They'd be crazy to try something like that. Especially not knowing that we redefined the meaning of the term *neighborhood watch*," Trevor laughed. "Relax. I'm going to make some ting to eat then we'll figure it out from ere. Cool?"

"Bet," Alvin said, somewhat relieved. He gazed out the window blankly, still trying to make heads or tails of his current dilemma. Trevor was being more than a gracious host by allowing him to stay at his home for the past few nights. Now all he needed to figure out was how he could safely enter back into society again. If there was such a chance. The first thing he needed to do was be sure the disks were stored away safely until he could straighten out this garbage. Trevor offered to guard the disks until he had time to clear his name with the Gumichi gang. Unfortunately, he knew time was no personal friend of his. Eventually, he would have to make a call to Franchesco and settle the confusion before the salt trickled out of his hour glass.

Hesitantly, Alvin picked up the cordless phone and punched in the seven digits. Upon hearing the familiar female voice on the answering service, he slammed the phone back in its cradle. *Where the hell is she?* Alvin flared. Celeste had never refused his calls before. Now that he needed her support, she managed to evade him.

Rolling his head around his neck, Alvin decided that a hot shower would relax him. Trevor was busy in the kitchen frying plantain and grooving to the sounds of Steel Pulse when Alvin announced, "I'm going up to take a shower."

Standing under the hot water gushing out of the copper shower nozzle, Alvin recited a quick prayer. Someone greater than him would have to save him from this deadly web. When it was safe, he and Trevor would run by the gym and pick up the disks from his locker. Then, he would have Trevor store them somewhere secure until it was time to face Franchesco. The thought of Tony hanging him out to be killed then tucked away in some new cement highway by Franchesco Gumichi, sent a surge of red flashing before his eyes.

Stepping out of the shower, Alvin peered into the foggy mirror. This whole ordeal unglued his faith in so called best friends. Studying his pupils for a few minutes, he eventually loosened up the wrinkles in his forehead. *If I ever get my hands on Tony Lucero,* Alvin swore to himself, *Franchesco Gumichi will have a guaranteed reason to come looking for me.*

Eight

"Celeste, I want you to move back home!" NaNe said vehemently. "Anything could happen to you at that apartment and the family wouldn't be able to get to you right away. You might as well pack your things and let me and Uncle Deak come and get you."

Celeste sat on the edge of Dante's bed with her eyes closed, momentarily. Why did she even bother to tell NaNe to begin with? Probably because Dante made her promise to tell her grandmother. And, since she never breaks her promises, she followed through like a fool. It was bad enough Dante forced her to move in with him for a while. But to have NaNe on her case as well was too much to deal with.

Throwing her hands up over her head, Celeste managed to break NaNe's sentence.

"NaNe," she whispered in a slow drawl. "I will be fine. I can't run away and hide this time. I have to deal with this."

"That's just plain simple Celeste!" NaNe said in a raised tone cutting off Celeste's sentence. "It doesn't make any sense for you to put yourself in a vulnerable position. Me and

Uncle Deak will be there this afternoon and that's that."

Celeste took a deep breath while the phone temporarily fell silent. For the first time in her life, she could feel herself wishing NaNe would back off and mind her own affairs this time.

"NaNe," she said as firmly as she could while maintaining a respectful tone. "That will not be necessary. Not now anyway. Dante has offered to let me to stay right at his place for a week or two, until we figure out what's going on. So, please, let's leave things like they are now. If something changes, I'll be sure to let you know."

Celeste could tell by NaNe's silence, she wasn't pleased with her tone much less her decision. Although NaNe silently acknowledged and respected her granddaughter's stubborn attitude, she still desperately wanted to come and whisk her away.

"Alright," NaNe exhaled. "Just promise me, you'll call me if you need me."

"I will NaNe. I promise."

"Good. Now what's Dante's number over there?"

Celeste let out a small laugh at her grandmother's relentless behavior. After rattling off the number, Celeste hung up the phone and lay back down on the bed. She didn't feel like going out into the ugly world today much less meeting Dante's mother, aunt and grandmother for dinner. What she impulsively craved, was to get back under the covers and go back to sleep.

This past week had been emotionally draining. The thought that Alvin was mixed up in something that could endanger her life was frightening. How selfish, she thought rolling over on her stomach. Once again, Alvin had only factored in his own emotions and self-fulfilling needs. Perhaps he'll learn a life value lesson from all this mess. Then again, maybe he wouldn't.

She could hear Dante's voice clearly now that the shower had stopped. She laughed. He was attempting to serenade himself with an old tune, "When A Man Loves A Woman." Thinking about the day that lay ahead of her, she truly didn't feel like being interrogated or looked over by his relatives today. But, she knew she had to face his folks and win their approval. Just like Dante, who had endured the awful questions by her relatives.

Looking around the bedroom, Celeste envisioned what it would be like to be married to Mr. Dante Lattimore. Dante's a neat freak, she decided, getting prepared to take her shower. Everything in his apartment had its place. And it stayed there too. The living room hosted his large thirty-one inch screen TV with surround sound VCR and stereo system. He had an enormous collection of videotapes. His CD collection also encompassed an array of artists. One thing she could say about Dante was that he had an affinity for music and movies. His bedroom favored a room right out of one of those Home Design magazines. The room was plastered with colors of black and white, and ranging in designs from checkers and stripes to plaids. There was a large black and white picture of Duke Ellington and Langston Hughes hanging behind the black leather sitting chair. The black cast iron bed had matching cast iron end tables. On one of the tables stood a crystal vase filled with fresh red roses, white and red candles in a crystal candle holder, and a Bible. The magazine basket held several GQ and EM magazines and a few hardcover books. Overall, Celeste adored Dante's taste.

Dante stood dripping wet, gazing at Celeste in the doorway. He was contemplating Celeste's permanent presence in his life. He always thought that the phrase, "Love at first sight" was an excuse people used to disguise their lustful feelings. But with Celeste, this cliché seemed true. Definitely something magnetic and real at their first encounter.

Dante had never seriously considered marriage even after Coach Johnson, his best buddy, ran the fast break down the church aisle. There had never been a woman in his life that moved him like Celeste did. He wanted her around—forever.

Dante walked up behind Celeste and planted a wet kiss on the nape of her neck. Celeste turned slowly. Her eyes clicked with his momentarily before she parted her full lips. "So, what do you think? Will your mom and aunts approve of me?"

"That depends," he grinned wrapping his arms around her waist.

"I'm serious," she said poking him in the chest. "Are they very protective of you? Are you a mama's boy?"

Dante broke the embrace between them, backing away slightly to get a better view of Celeste. He could sense her anxiety about meeting his family. Actually, she would be safer, more comfortable with facing his mother and his aunts than with his father, if he had still been alive.

"Celeste, don't worry, all right? My aunts and my mother are like tigers with no teeth or claws. They may look intimidating but believe me, they're not. They are very active in the church and strongly believe in the Lord. They remind me of NaNe in that way. Whatever you do just don't lead on that we're living together permanently. 'Cause if you do, they're liable to jump up and lay hands on you right there. Relax. I'll be there for you just like you were there for me with your family," he smiled raising an eyebrow.

"Yeah right. I know what that means," she chuckled. "You're going to leave me for the wolves like you accused me of doing to you with my family. Anyway, if I get in a jam, all I have to do is tell them how well you wiggle them hips. That should keep things calm," she laughed, walking toward the bathroom.

"Really? And how would you remember? I think it's more of a rolling motion. But then, of course, if you need me to show you again so that it'll be clearer to you, I can," he whispered following her.

Celeste stopped in the bathroom doorway and egged, "That won't be necessary. You'd better save your strength. I wouldn't want your mom blaming me for exhausting you this morning." She flipped on the shower.

"Celeste, as you will soon learn, I have a lot of strength," he murmured stepping into the tub behind her and yanking the shower curtain closed.

Celeste and Dante arrived at the small brick home promptly at 5:00pm. Once reaching the top of the stairs, Celeste gasped lightly, trying to suck in additional air. She needed to slow her heart rate down and the only way to do that was to take a deep breath or two. Fluffing the bottom of her dress out she let it fall back into place. The long, loose-fitting, raw silk, turquoise summer dress highlighted her beautiful complexion. She wore a soft rust, matte lipstick that picked up the orange-berry colored blush. The gold and turquoise clip-on earrings set the finishing touch on her outfit. If God was on her side, like He always had been, things would sail along smoothly. This was a big day for Dante and her. Meeting the matriarchs of his family and gaining their insight would serve as a true measure of any future they could have together.

Dante held the screen door open so that Celeste could go ahead of him. He was such the gentleman, she thought to herself. He was clean and crisp in his white linen outfit. As they stepped into the foyer, a tall, medium-built, bronze-complected woman greeted them. She had on an African fabric smock with a matching skirt. Her loosely curled hair was cut in a short natural. A pair of long tiger's-eye earrings dangled from her tiny ears.

"Mom," Dante sang, pausing briefly to look his mother over then giving her a hug. "You look beautiful mom. Is this one of your new designs?" he asked feeling the material.

"This old thing? Heavens no. I've had this for awhile," she responded, glancing past Dante and fixing her gaze upon Celeste.

"You must be Celeste," she smiled walking past her son. "I'm Lydia Lattimore." She extended her hand.

"It's a pleasure to meet you Mrs. Lattimore." Celeste grinned.

"Please, call me Lydia. Everyone else does. I see no reason to be formal."

Their eyes locked for a while longer before the other family members interrupted. Mrs. Lattimore wanted to assess her son's new found paramour and determine if she would be an asset or a liability to his life. The one thing she didn't want Dante to do was give his heart to someone who didn't deserve it. She'd be able to detect Celeste's true intentions before the day was over. She was sure of it.

Three other woman and two men appeared in the foyer to greet Dante with hugs, kisses and handshakes. His Aunt Karlene, his mother's sister, and her brother Derrick, his uncle, who was married to Sandra, and his grandmother Leona and her second husband Bruce, were all standing in the hallway. Dante grabbed Celeste by the hand and led her into the small crowd.

"This lovely lady is my sweetheart, Celeste. Celeste, this is my family." He introduced Celeste to everyone as they all made their way back into the large family room. He sat down in the loveseat next to the fireplace beside Celeste. Mrs. Lattimore sat in the leather chair on the opposite side of Dante. Sandra and Derrick sat on the other loveseat while Leona, Bruce and Karlene sat on the antique white sofa facing Celeste and Dante.

Dante laughed. "What's on the menu this evening? I'm starving."

"Your mama and I put together your favorite dish— succotash," Karlene replied.

"Yes, and your grandmother baked a honey-glazed ham and some of her home-made dinner rolls," his mother said smiling. "I also baked a chocolate cake and threw together some red beans and rice, and macaroni and cheese."

"Sounds good," Dante grinned looking at Celeste.

"What about you, Celeste?" Karlene asked.

"I hope you like what's on the menu for the evening."

"Yes," Celeste smiled. "There are things on the menu I eat." She'd have to make the best of it even if she didn't eat pork or beans. This was an important day. She didn't want to cast a shadow over it by making an issue about the menu. Basically, she appreciated their efforts and hospitality however stiff it seemed.

"Praise the Lord for that. Child, you look like you're the picky sort that lives only on that there rabbit food they sell in the health food store," Leona murmured struggling to get up off the sofa.

"Celeste," Lydia said leaning forward in her chair and speaking across Dante. "My son tells me you're studying to become a dentist. Your family must be very proud of you."

"Yes, that's right. I'll be graduating in May and can't wait. Neither can my family members. Matter of fact, they have already purchased an appointment book for me and scheduled their appointments in for the next year."

The laughter was certainly appreciated and helped to loosen up the atmosphere.

"Perhaps we should do the same thing," Derrick said jokingly.

"Fifty one years young and I have never had a filling," Lydia smiled.

"Wow!" Celeste said leaning forward trying to get a better view of Lydia's mouth. She had perfectly straight teeth that were shiny white. "You certainly have beautiful teeth. And, you've obviously taken excellent care of them. Who is your dentist?"

"Doctor Robinson," Dante cut in. "You remember me telling you about my first visit with her as a child. How I yelled and screamed until mother came in and gave me one of her looks."

"Oh that story," Celeste laughed shaking her head. "You were probably a dentist's worst nightmare," she smiled touching Dante on the hand playfully.

"That may have been true then, but I'm sure I'm more of a daydream for some other dentist," he smirked grabbing her hand.

"Awh, isn't that cute," Sandra said elbowing Derrick.

"Yes it sure is," Karlene stated wryly. "So, when's the big day?"

Celeste felt her cheeks grow warm and her heart flutter. She averted her gaze away from Karlene to Sandra. In that quick amount of time, she was able to assess that Sandra was the true romantic of the family. She was thankful for Dante's quick, suave response.

"I'm not really sure," Dante said catching Celeste off guard. "We'll have to wait and see how things move along. Huh, sweetheart?" he said squeezing Celeste's hand.

"Exactly," Celeste responded.

"You mean to tell me you're considering marriage?" Lydia asked with a raised brow. "How long has it been since the two of you've been dating?"

"Seems like all of our lives to me. What about

you darling? Seem like an eternity to you, too?" Dante said looking at Celeste. He didn't wait for Celeste to respond. Instead, he turned toward his mother, placed his left hand on her hand and smiled, "Don't get all bent out of shape, mother. We're still in the early stages of our relationship. Relax."

"I'm not getting bent out of shape. I just don't want to be left in the dark. Or hear that you have eloped. Dante, you're my only son and that would break my heart. Don't let him do that you hear me, Celeste?" she said seriously.

"We won't Mrs. Lattimore. Don't worry. I couldn't face you or my grandmother if we ran off and got married," she laughed.

"Now see Dante," Lydia said pointing to Celeste. "We could always make room in the family for another smart woman."

Celeste blushed at the unexpected compliment. She hadn't pegged Mrs. Lattimore as the accolade-giving type but she guessed she was wrong. Dante kissed Celeste's hand, looked around the room at each of his relatives and said, "Good. Cause you just very well may have to make room for Celeste if things continue to go as beautifully as they are."

Light conversation passed before everyone shifted their positions from the living area to the dining room table. The table was set with fine china, silver flatware and crystal glasses, which were offset with a beautiful bouquet of exotic, fresh flowers. Lydia orchestrated the seating arrangements. She sat at the head of one end of the table while she instructed Dante to sit at the other end. Celeste sat to Dante's left, next to Sandra and Derrick. Leona sat on Lydia's left, next to Bruce. Karlene was seated to Dante's right and directly facing Celeste.

"Son, since you're the head of my family now, would you lead us in a prayer?"

"Sure mother. Everyone hold hands please." Dante recited a prayer.

"That was a beautiful prayer, Dante," Celeste beamed squeezing his hand.

"Thank you, baby," he replied locking eyes with her momentarily.

"He always has meaningful prayers, dear," Karlene said proudly.

Dinner turned out to be a raving success with Celeste charming everyone, including Leona and Karlene, with her gifted sense of humor and exuding concern for humankind. Though the red beans and rice were a little hard for her to swallow, Celeste managed to force them down anyway to save face. Things had gone so well that Leona invited Dante and Celeste over to dinner the Sunday after next. Also, Celeste learned that Karlene, Lydia's baby sister, had lost her husband in a car accident a few years ago. That explained why she appeared so callous, so apathetic and so reclusive.

After discussing the plight of animals as it related to fur coats, Celeste realized Karlene was a loving person, who found it easier to hide behind her wall of fear and unaddressed pain. Perhaps Celeste would introduce her to Uncle Deak. Lydia, also an elementary teacher, was familiar with NaNe and her reputation as an excellent teacher. Overall, what appeared to be a rocky beginning between Dante and his family, turned out to be a smooth sail.

Celeste laid her head back against the headrest of the car and let out a deep sigh, "What a time. Dinner was nice."

"Yeah. Do you think we're moving too fast?" Dante asked out of the blue.

"I feel like things are moving at the pace they're supposed to. Only God truly knows where the path will lead."

"I enjoy being with you so much. I only hope the feeling is mutual," he said caressing her hand.

"As it stands right now Dante, I can't think of anyone else I'd rather be with. What about you? Do you feel things are moving too fast?"

"Honestly, my sweetness," he said glancing over at Celeste. "I think things are progressing the way they're supposed to. I just hope I can keep up with my heart," he grinned.

"Is that so Mr. Lattimore?" she said cupping his hand. She truly prayed that this man was the real thing, having all the qualities she'd prayed for. God, she heard her mind say, I must be in love with this man.

Nine

Labor Day weekend passed quickly before Celeste and Dante realized it. They had gone down to Stone Mountain, Georgia outside of Atlanta for a few days to get away. They arrived at the quaint log cabin late Friday evening. On Saturday morning, Dante cooked a gourmet breakfast and served Celeste in bed. Then, he pulled out his black bag, laid the pedicure instruments, massage oil and peppermint foot lotion out and proceeded to give Celeste the pedicure of her life.

Later that evening, they headed into the city for dinner and some live jazz. They spent half of Sunday on a small boat, fishing, talking, and sunbathing. Celeste had packed some smoked turkey, wheat crackers, port-wine cheese, grapes, strawberries, sparkling cider and spring water in a cooler for their secluded cruise. On Sunday evening, they relaxed in an outdoor Jacuzzi, taking turns giving each other massages.

The weekend was a blast, Dante reminisced, as he made the left onto Main Street. All he had aimed to do this past weekend was to ensure that Celeste would be fully relaxed before she began her rigorous school schedule tomorrow. After the twelve hour drive, he had worked up a taste for some home-made ice-cream.

"How does ice cream sound to top off our weekend?" he asked pulling forward into the parking space.

"You've been reading my mind again," she said tiredly. The drive home in the direct sunlight had zapped her energy.

"What did I tell you before darling? There's no such thing as reading minds. We just have what I'd call a spiritual connection, that's all," he said stepping out of the car. "Plainly put, the Lord just put us together. What's that verse that says a man should leave his father and mother, and take a wife? Well, I've got half of the verse complete," he grinned.

"Not just any wife, you know? You have to get one who's spiritually-grounded and evenly yoked, honest, sincere, respectful, sexually gratifying and loyal. But most importantly, one who will be clocking dollars. You know, like me," she chuckled tickling him upon entering the store.

The ice cream parlor was cramped with college students returning from their summer break. Dante and Celeste felt like an old couple of parents bouncing into an oversized playpen. Dante reached back and embraced Celeste's hand. Trudging through the crowd, he led her up the narrow stairs to a table by the back window overlooking the cobblestone alley.

The waiter approached the table and in a rushed tone huffed, "What'll it be this evening?"

Celeste glanced at Dante then back at the waiter. In that quick amount of time, she had made her decision. "I'll have the strawberry shortcake."

Dante smiled widely at Celeste's choice. "What? Straying away from our healthy menu?"

"Be quiet, Dante. I'm sure if you were really that concerned about my diet, you wouldn't have brought me here in the first place. So don't even try it," she smiled.

The waiter shifted waiting for Dante's decision. "Hmm, let's see. I think I'll have the double chocolate cake with two scoops of vanilla ice cream." The waiter snatched the pen from behind his ear, jotted the orders down on the memo pad and hurried away.

"You probably should get two scoops of vanilla yogurt before I have to refer to you as Chunky Lattimore," she mumbled under her breath jokingly.

"What did you say?" he smirked, dipping his fingers in his glass of water then flicking the water toward Celeste's face. "Don't make me have to show everybody in this place who's in charge," he laughed.

She let out a soft snicker, reached into her red handbag and drew out a small water gun. She returned the gesture by squirting him in the face with some water. Before Celeste had time to move the gun away from Dante's hand, he had snatched the gun from her. "Now," he said leaning back in the chair with the water gun aimed at her face. "Who's the man?"

Celeste was giggling out of control. Dante leaned over to her and pressed his face real close to hers and threatened, "Stop laughing. You better stop laughing before I spray you," he teased playfully. But Celeste couldn't gain her composure.

The waiter returned with their plates in the nick of time to save Celeste from a complete showering. He had the check tucked under his left arm. Placing the dish in front of them, the waiter dropped the check on the edge of the table and disappeared.

After a few bites of strawberries, Celeste's eyes perused the room. It wasn't until her eyes came full circle again that she recognized the tall figure standing at the top of the stairs. Their eyes locked briefly before Celeste nodded. Dante followed her gaze until his eyes became level with the thin brother walking toward their table.

"Celeste," Alvin said flatly. "Glad to see you're still breathing since you never returned any of my calls."

"Alvin," Celeste replied just as flatly. Silence hovered over the table like a cloud looming over a mountain. Dante frowned as his eyes stayed fixed on Alvin. Celeste hadn't bumped into him since the jazz concert at the early part of summer. Dante had a few questions for Alvin. Was he the one responsible for the mess at Celeste's apartment? If so, why would he jeopardize her? He strained to keep his cool. However, Alvin was intent on harassing Celeste.

"How come you haven't returned my calls, Celeste? What? Two-three years between us and you don't care what happens to me now that you've found somebody else?"

"Listen Alvin," she said strongly. "I do care about what happens to you, but things are different between us now. Besides, how did I know all those messages weren't another one of your ploys? You've acted so strangely towards me these past few months, I don't know what to think."

Alvin could feel his face turning colors as his temperature began to swell. How dare she try to act so matter of fact with him. If it hadn't been for him, her little ass and her dream to become a dentist would be just that. A dream. "Pardon me a minute brother while I have a word with Celeste," he said looking down at Dante. Dante didn't budge. He just sneered at Alvin while their eyes cinched together.

Celeste sat in her chair trying to figure out a way to keep these two from fighting. "Look Alvin, let's just let it go. I apologize for not returning your calls, but do try to understand things from where I'm sitting."

"Excuse me, Celeste, but I think that's bullshit, plain and simple. It crushed my heart to think that you couldn't give a damn about a simple thing like my welfare."

"Okay," Dante snapped standing up so suddenly that his chair fell over. "That's enough man. You're looking just fine to us, so why don't you drop it and go on about your life?"

"My problem is not with you, man," Alvin said shaking his head from side to side. "That's why I politely asked you to excuse us while I got my thoughts off my mind."

"Yeah?" Dante said thumping Alvin's chest. "Maybe you could explain to this sweet woman why someone ransacked her apartment."

Alvin shot a fast glance at Celeste and replied, "What? What do you mean somebody was looking for something in your apartment? Are you all right? When did this happen? How come you didn't call me?" The questions were rolling out of his mouth faster than he could take his next breath.

Celeste stared at Alvin blankly. Actually, she was studying his face, his body language, his question. From all she had learned about Alvin over the years, she knew he was involved in some way. Her heart sank at the thought that Alvin would even participate in something that could possibly endanger her life, or anyone else's for that matter.

"What difference does it make now? Nobody was hurt and nothing was taken. Whoever did it was in a hurry and searching for something that Celeste obviously didn't have,"

Dante said somberly. "Perhaps you want to shed some light on the situation?"

Alvin cut a look at Dante, then replied, "Who the hell are you to be questioning me?"

"Believe me. You'll find out soon enough. I'm only going to say this once. If anything so much as frightens Celeste in her sleep, I'm coming to look for you."

"Don't threaten me," Alvin shouted. "Boy, you don't know who you're dealing with or what you're dealing with. So you better mind your own damn business. Matter of fact, you keep your eyes peeled too!" Alvin snapped backing away. He moved toward the stairs, eyes flaming. Once he could feel the banister, he turned and walked down the stairs. Dante walked over to the balcony and followed Alvin's strides until he left the store. He was going to take care of this low life soon. But he had to be patient. At least for a little while longer.

Alvin slammed the door behind him so hard that it rattled the clay vase sitting on the coffee table. Trevor ran down the stairs two at a time with his shotgun wedged under his right arm.

"Damn mon. What the hell is going on? I done tink somebody broke into the crib," Trevor said lowering the gun. "What's up?"

Alvin plopped on the sofa then let his face fall in his hands. After a few seconds, he lifted his head, cleared his throat and replied, "I saw

Celeste at the creamery. She was with that punk boyfriend of hers," he said standing. "He had the nerve to threaten me. Can you believe that?"

"So what you want to do? Want to give him a lesson?" Trevor smirked.

"Yeah, he's got it coming but that's not my immediate concern now. Do you know Gumichi and his thugs trashed Celeste's apartment?"

"Say what? You serious?"

"Yes, unfortunately. Man I'm going to have to get this nonsense under control and soon before things really get out of hand." Alvin let out a deep sigh, then leaned back on the sofa. The thought of Gumichi's gruntmen going to Celeste's home angered him. What if she had been there? What if they had done something to her? Then his thoughts took a different direction. If they could find her so quickly it was only a matter of time before they caught up to him. He would have to square up this business as soon as possible before somebody seriously got hurt.

"When do you want to pick the diskettes up from the gym?" Trevor asked.

"Soon. Real soon. Perhaps later this week. After we get a plan, of course. Trevor, I've got a funny feeling and I don't like it. Let's put our heads together in the morning. By then I'll have cooled off."

"All right. Just let me know," Trevor said standing up. "I'm going back to sleep. I've got a long day ahead of me. And from the way it sounds, I may have a long week ahead of me too. Good night."

"Good night," Alvin mumbled. His blood was still baking from the scene at the ice cream store a few hours ago. Too many thoughts were swimming in his head. Maybe he should turn in for the night. There was nothing much else he could accomplish tonight. As he turned off the living room lights and headed up the stairs, another thought raced through his mind. *What did that brother mean when he said I'll find out soon enough? Who the hell is he anyway?* He'd have to do some digging of his own.

Ten

Celeste had a difficult time adjusting to the new semester. She needed the entire week to get acclimated to studying again. After spending the past few weeks on a mental vacation, she had to battle with her mind to remain focused in class. Her life with Dante during the past few months made her wish all the more that she was completely done with dental school.

The campus at Howard University was crawling with hundreds of students as she walked through the yard toward W Street. Students ranged in ages from a tender eighteen years old to a mature forty years or more. The demographic contributions of the students were responsible for Howard's diverse population. On any given day, a student new to town could undoubtedly find a homeboy or homegirl from their neck of the woods. It didn't matter if a person was from the motor city, the Big Apple, Oak-Town, Chi-Town, Africa, Barbados, NAP or South Central. You could always locate someone from the city of your choice at Howard University.

Dante was scheduled to pick her up in ten minutes behind the Dental School building. She would have to walk a lot faster if she was going to get there on time. Her long, denim skirt and medium-heeled platform shoes didn't help her situation none either. She could feel her heartbeat pounding with each step and realized she was beginning to panic unnecessarily. Dante had become very protective of her since the break in at her apartment and the scene with Alvin. She was beginning to feel a little bit smothered. Not really, she negated the thought quickly. She knew his intentions were harmless and genuine.

She reached the rear of the building just as Dante pulled up. He popped out of the car in a pair of jeans, a matching denim shirt and a funky denim Redskins baseball cap. "Hey babe," he gleamed wrapping his large arms around her back. "How was your day?"

"Tiring. I can't seem to concentrate in class. My mind just wanders all over the place," she replied while Dante opened her car door.

"I read something about your mind-wandering syndrome today somewhere. I believe the doctors attributed it to getting old," he laughed closing her door before she had a chance to respond.

Celeste laughed as he got in on the driver's side. "You missed your calling Dante. You know that?" she said reaching over and placing a wet smack on his cheek. "That's why I've fallen so hard for you. You've got the greatest sense of humor sugarcoating your wonderful personality. Thanks for bumping into me that day," she grinned.

"Bumping into you? The way I recall it you were attempting to live out that phrase, *I am woman hear me roar,* trying to carry five boxes at once. Yeah I did the bumping all right."

They stole a glimpse of each other, then snickered. The one thing Dante appreciated about Celeste was her playful spirit and sense of humor. He loved seeing her laugh and made it a daily goal to keep her in stitches.

"You're going to NaNe's right?"

"Yup," she mumbled while looking into the sunvisor's mirror and reapplying her red matte lipstick. She ran her tongue over her teeth to wipe away any traces of the red. "My cousin Iris is waiting for me at NaNe's. She's visiting from Europe for a few weeks."

"Iris?" Dante said wrinkling his forehead trying to place the name. "Oh yeah, that's your Uncle Deak's daughter. The model. When's the last time you two saw each other?"

"Gosh, Christmas past. I guess. Anyway, how was your day? Anything exciting you want to tell me about?"

"Not really. Overall my day has been uneventful. That is, until I saw your precious face," he smiled pinching her lightly on the cheek. He turned onto NaNe's block. "Another relative to meet?" he yawned. "I don't think I can take much more of this," he teased while parking the car.

NaNe had the white screen door with the little black handle locked. Celeste placed her face on the mesh screen and peered into the house. She rang the bell a second time before she heard NaNe's thunderous footsteps hit the hard wood floors.

"Little Bit," NaNe sang joyously in her purple apron. " 'Bout time you two got here. I was starting to worry. Hello, Dante," she said kissing them each on the forehead. "Come on in. Iris is upstairs cleaning up. You kids hungry? I just pulled a peach cobbler out of the oven ten minutes ago. Have some," she said, walking back to the kitchen.

"Maybe later NaNe. Thank you," Celeste said dropping her bag on the kitchen bench.

"What about you, Dante? I know you want to try some of NaNe's famous cobbler."

"You don't have to twist my arm, NaNe," he glowed.

NaNe got a large bowl out of the cabinet. She scooped out a large portion of the hot, juicy cobbler and plopped it in the bowl. Celeste noticed Dante's mouth watering as NaNe placed the bowl down in front of him.

"I have some Breyer's vanilla ice cream to go over that if you'd like."

"Yes ma'am," Dante happily replied, glancing at his lady love. Celeste cracked a faint smile, then shook her head. How in the world would she be able to keep up with Dante's accelerated metabolism? Just then, she noticed

her cousin Iris standing in the kitchen archway.

"Iris," she said vibrantly, skipping over to
greet her.

"Celeste," Iris screamed running over to
meet her half way. The two embraced for a
few moments before Celeste backed away.

"Look at you girl! You look great!" Celeste
proclaimed turning her cousin around then
looking her up and down. She had to stretch
her neck a bit to get a good look at her cousin's
head. Iris stood some four inches above her 5'6,
brickhouse-framed cousin, Celeste.

"Thank you. You look wonderful yourself,"
Iris said with a slight European accent. "And
who is the young gent?" Iris whispered. "He
looks a lot different from the man I've seen
in your life for the past few years."

"My God Iris. Has it been that long?" Celeste
let out a deep breath and continued, "I'll have
to fill you in later. Dante," she said pulling her
cousin by the hand over to the table. Dante
dropped his spoon in the bowl and stood up.
"This is my favorite cousin and my best buddy,
Iris. Iris this is my new beau, Dante."

"Pleased to meet you," Dante said shaking
her hand. *Damn!* he heard his mind say. *She's
a taller version of Celeste. No wonder everyone is
raving about Iris, she looks exactly like Celeste. The
resemblance is startling.* He knew he was staring.
But he couldn't help himself. He had heard
that every person had a twin somewhere in
the world, but this was scary.

"Same here," Iris smiled. "I see NaNe has you addicted to her cooking already. I guess it'll be hard to get rid of you now, won't it?"

Everyone laughed then took their places. Dante returned to his peach cobbler a la mode, which was now a sopping bowl of cream. NaNe continued nurturing the pots on the stove and Celeste and Iris got lost in their own conversation. Midway through their talk, Celeste noticed the sparkling diamond wrapped around Iris' left ring finger. "What's this?" she asked grabbing Iris' left hand. "You got engaged and you didn't tell me? I should strangle you girl," Celeste teased. "How long have you been keeping this secret?"

"Actually, it's my wedding ring," Iris replied lowly.

"Your what? You're kidding right?"

"Sshh," Iris gestured pointing to NaNe. "I haven't told anybody yet. They think I'm engaged. I need to break the news to Daddy but he won't be back from New York until tomorrow."

Celeste raised her eyebrows and fell silent. What the hell had Iris done?

"I'll tell you about it later. Okay?"

No, it wasn't okay, Celeste determined. How could her favorite cousin, her best buddy go and do something so monumental and not clue her in?

Dante rose from his plate and made his way over to them. "Excuse me, sweetheart. I hate to interrupt the welcoming party but I've got to go," he said bending down to kiss her on the cheek. "It was nice meeting you, Iris. How long you in the country for?"

"A few weeks. I'm sure I'll be seeing you again. Take care of my cousin."

"You better believe it," he smiled, then walked over to NaNe and gave her a kiss and hug. Celeste accompanied him to the front door while Iris followed behind.

"Bye Dante," Iris waved heading up the stairs. "Celeste come on up when you're done so we can have a session."

Celeste slipped into Dante's arms then laid her head on his chest. He squeezed and kissed her on the lips. "You staying the night here or do you want me to pick you up later?"

"I think I'm going to stay here for the night. Iris and I will probably go shopping in the morning. What if I call you tomorrow and let you know what's going on?"

"Fine. You know how to reach me," he said. "Be safe sweetheart."

"I will. And you be safe, too. And hey," she said calling behind him out the door. "I know it's Friday night but try to steer clear of the hoochie mamas all right?"

"Got it baby. You know you're the only mama for me."

Celeste locked the screen door and closed the oak door behind him. She told NaNe she and Iris would be upstairs.

"Now what the heck is going on?" Celeste frowned as she entered the tiny room and lay down on the twin, maple bed across from her cousin. "You must be very happy Mrs. . . . ?"

"Santini," Iris said finishing Celeste's sentence. "As a matter of fact, I'm happier than I've ever been with Tom."

"Tom Santini? That's an unusual name for a brother."

Iris looked away from Celeste and said, "He's mostly Italian with a little French in him."

There was an intense moment of silence. Celeste was reflecting on Iris' previous relationships while they were growing up. Iris' decision really didn't surprise Celeste. She could remember Iris dating only two brothers in her entire life: Jermaine Roberts while in high school and Derrick Lang during her first three years at college. After that time, Iris found it more appealing to spend her time with men from a variety of ethnic backgrounds. The family had never made a fuss over Iris' choice of male companions. Usually because she would manage to date men with some type of African heritage. Celeste could recall her cousin's dating repertoire as something like this: a young handsome gent from Morocco, a tall wealthy man from Spain and an eccentric but well-educated man from Greece.

Celeste took a deep breath then exhaled, "How long have you known him?"

Iris' gaze set upon her cousin's full face once again. "A year."

"How old is he?"

"Fifty two."

"What? Fifty two! How in the hell did you get wrapped up with someone who's Uncle Deak's age?"

Iris shrugged her shoulders and let out a tiny smile. "I'm sure it has something to do with his bank account."

Celeste shook her head in disbelief because she knew the task that lay ahead of her cousin would be difficult. Just how would Iris break the news to her father? She let out a grunt under her breath and continued. "What does he do?"

"He's an architect and owns an architectural design firm in Switzerland. You should see some of his work Celeste. It's breathtaking."

"Perhaps seeing his bank account would be more breath taking," she grinned.

"He won't admit exactly how much he earns. I have seen some documents lying around the house. And I know for a fact he makes well over a million dollars a year," she giggled. "Now what kind of man here in the States could provide that kind of security for me?"

Celeste frowned at her cousin's negative statement. "Don't go there Iris. It's not necessary. Just remember your papa didn't have a million dollars to blanket you with but he had unconditional love. And he gave you whatever he had."

"I know that, Celeste. I didn't mean to imply anything about Daddy. So don't get worked up. I guess I've become adjusted to a different degree of living, of expectations. That's all I meant by my statement."

"You're still digging a hole for yourself, cuz. Best we change the subject all right? I mean for you to even insinuate that there is nothing a man could do for you unless his pockets run deep, sounds totally ludicrous to me."

Iris replied, "I don't dislike anyone, no matter what their complexion or ethnic heritage. I'm concerned about money. Sorry if I feel that some of the men here have oversized egos that don't match anywhere near their undersized wallets. They think it's okay to stand on one of their legs and mooch off the women with their other one. Celeste, do you mean to tell me you would really marry for love only? Are you saying you would allow someone to be a part of your life who doesn't come to the table with at least the same or more of what you have to offer?"

"First of all Iris, if the man respects me, is progressive in his life's goals, and if he can be supportive of me and my aspirations and care for me unconditionally, I would give him my heart. Would it matter if he was broke? Of course it would. However, if he's achieved some of his goals and has set new ones to accomplish, then we have something to work with. Would I mind if his bank account was swollen? Absolutely not. Would I penalize him if his account was like mine, fairly empty? I don't think so, darling."

"Yeah, well, I have a new lifestyle now. And I need money to support it. I'll go for whoever has the most green." Iris laughed.

This conversation was heading nowhere, Celeste resolved quietly. *Sometimes Iris pisses me off to no return with all her high and mighty, unsubstantiated opinions.*

NaNe's presence in the doorway halted their conversation. She was standing with her hands on her hips and a towel draped over her left shoulder. "What you girls in such a fuss about? I can tell you've been in some type of heated discussion because you both look a bit fried in the face." NaNe waited for some type of explanation that would address her comment but she got nothing but silence.

"Have it your way then. All I know is you two better remember you're family. No matter what happens. You all better brand that in your memory," she advised walking back down the stairs.

Iris looked at her cousin then asked, "Enough about the money issue, Celeste. How have things been for you? I see you have a new man. Is Alvin on the permanent disabled list or is he just vacationing?"

Celeste gathered her attitude together then let out a tiny sigh. Iris always had a way with words but since her years as a resident in Europe, her ability to linguistically diversify her sentences had become more intriguing.

"He's gone. Dante is the new brother in my life now."

"I see. And how long have you two been an item?"

"Five months," Celeste grinned.

"Are you in love with him?"

"As a matter of fact, I am. I didn't want to fall in love with him so soon. Especially after the break-up with Alvin, but things just clicked from day one. We've had a few disagreements but nothing mind blowing. He's such a wonderful brother, Iris. There is nothing he would not do for me. He's considerate, supportive, compassionate, a well-bred gentleman and he respects me." She emphasized respect. "If things continue at this pace, I think I could consider marrying him."

"Why wait? Do you think you could marry him now?"

Celeste placed her hands behind her head and lay back against the pillows. She had never considered marrying anyone this quickly but then again not everyone was Dante Lattimore. "I suppose I could. I don't know, it's too soon."

"Says who? You? Dante? Society? Or NaNe? Who is really governing your life choices, Celeste?" Iris was meaning to imply NaNe. Ever since she could remember, Celeste always seemed to care what NaNe thought about her decisions. Something Iris felt was restricting for her cousin. Simply put, Iris kept to herself, it was time for Celeste to pop the apron strings from NaNe. From where Iris was sitting she saw her cousin as a thirty-two year old woman living a life of a sixty-year old. She would have to find a way to keep NaNe's influence out of her decision making process. "Well," she said waiting for her cousin's answer.

"Says me. I guess. It just seems too soon to consider marrying someone who you've known for only a few months. How about you? How long did you and Tom wait?"

"Seven weeks."

"Seven weeks! My God Iris, what was the rush? Was it your idea or his?"

"It was a mutual decision. We decided that it felt right and we didn't want to chance losing one another."

"Then you've been married for almost a year. Girl, how are you going to tell your dad?"

"I just am. He'll either accept it or he won't. What am I supposed to do? Besides, Tom will be in town in a couple of days to meet him. We'll work it out. I'm sure of it. That's neither here nor there. The main thing right now is to make sure you don't let the opportunity for happiness with someone special pass you by because of some societal or familial protocol. Just do your thing, girl. You always have. What you need to concentrate on is disintegrating that apron string with you and NaNe. I'm sure one of the reasons for you and Alvin's split had to do with NaNe's constant buzzing in your ear."

Celeste nodded her head in acknowl-
edgment of her cousin's advice. She knew Iris
had a valid point. But no one understood her
relationship with NaNe but her. The truth of
the matter was, she appreciated NaNe's wisdom and experience. Maybe the delivery of
her messages was abrasive at times but overall,
NaNe is a wise woman with an extraordinary
gift from God. Very rarely is NaNe wrong
about her feelings, her visions. Over protective
perhaps but hardly incorrect. Especially about
Alvin Brouchard.

Eleven

5:30 a.m. The little green numbers on the Sony clock radio caught Celeste's attention when she rolled over on her side. Slowly, she searched for Dante's silhouette. She hadn't slept well because she was preoccupied with meeting Iris and her husband, Tom, at NaNe's for brunch this morning. It wasn't until she heard the whisper from the other room that she realized that Dante was not lying next to her. From what she could gather from his part of the conversation, he was planning to "handle the situation today." And that "all systems were a go."

She strained her ears as hard as she could to hear more of the conversation but couldn't. Dante was speaking very low and muffled. Sitting up in the bed, Celeste began to feel irritated and suspicious. *Who in God's name could he be talking to at this hour?* she pondered. Furthermore, what situation was he talking about handling today? Hastily, she lay her head back down on the feather pillow when she heard Dante hang up the phone. She eased back into a pretentious state of sleep, while he stood at her side of the bed peering down at her. He would never let anything or anyone take her away from him, he vowed placing a kiss on her cheek. "I love you Celeste Dunbar," he murmured in her ear biting her lobe lightly.

The shower was running full steam when Celeste slipped out of the bed and tip-toed into the livingroom. Glancing around the room, she didn't notice anything out of the ordinary. The phone sat on the coffee table next to Dante's gym bag. On the opposite side of the bag, she noticed a pad with the name Rough House and the initials T.L. A.B. She fingered through the partly opened gym bag looking for more clues. A sign that would provide her with information about Dante's early morning conversation. Neatly folded near the top of the bag was a green sweat shirt with a thick hood. Tucked underneath the shirt lay a pair of sweat pants and a pair of white cotton socks. Letting her hand rummage around the bottom of the bag, she bumped into a cold, metal object. Carefully, she pushed the clothing to one side to get a closer view of the hard object. She took a sudden step back and gasped, when she saw the large, black gun with the initials K.O.D.Y. engraved near the handle. Then the water to the shower stopped. *My Lord!* She ran past the bathroom door and dove into the bed. Her heart was racing wildly as she battled to control her breathing. *Calm down girl. Come on,* she said to herself. A few seconds later, the bathroom door swung open.

Celeste didn't move. She was scared and shocked. *Why would Dante be carrying a gun? And why were the initials K.O.D.Y. etched in the gun?* she wondered.

Suddenly, Celeste felt a surge of emotions overcoming her. Why hadn't Dante mentioned to her that there was a gun in the house? And who the hell is KODY anyhow? She almost yelled when Dante placed his lips on her shoulder. She moaned lightly in an attempt to make her disguise about sleeping seem real.

"I'm going down to the gym and then meet some of the players for lunch later. I'll call you at NaNe's. Love you," he said walking down the hallway. Celeste opened her eyes after the familiar click of the front door closing. She sat on the corner of the bed, staring at the picture of Langston Hughes. Her mind was racing in a dozen directions. *He was going to the gym now?* she questioned aloud. It just didn't set right with her. Replaying this morning's moments, she couldn't understand one other thing. *Who in their right mind would take a shower before they went to work out?*

Alvin Brouchard picked up the phone and began dialing Celeste's phone number. Disgusted, he jammed the phone back in its cradle when he heard her answering machine pick up. It had been five months since their break-up and a month since he had seen her last. He really wished that he could redo the scene at the ice cream parlor again. But, oh well, it was too late now. Alvin had more pressing matters at hand. Like trying to straighten things out with Tony and his uncle. Luckily, he had been able to shake Gumichi and his thugs for three weeks. But now time was trickling down and they were getting closer with their trail.

Alvin looked at the phone once more. He needed to talk to Celeste right now. He had to make her understand and believe that his only dream was to secure a future for them financially. That's all. He wanted to tell her how right she was about Tony Lucero and how unreliable he had been after all. Honestly, Alvin desired to have Celeste back in his life, in his corner. If not as his lover, then certainly as his best friend.

Tying the shoelaces on his sneakers, he took a moment to reflect on the happy moments they had shared during their three year relationship. The memories caused a smile to creep over his lips as he sat on the edge of the bed with his hands on his knees. The fondest memory and the most sentimental thought he honed in on was last Thanksgiving Day. He was bedridden with a severe case of the flu, and Celeste had managed to save the day. It had snowed in the nation's capital, surprising and inhibiting a number of D.C. residents that day. NaNe had prepared a family spread and was expecting everyone to attend come hell or high water. Celeste phoned NaNe to say she would be unable to attend Thanksgiving dinner because Alvin was ill. Needless to say, NaNe split a vein, ranting and raving about it being a family day and Celeste should be here cause after all, Alvin isn't family anyhow. But Celeste stood firm, denying NaNe's smoked turkey and home-made stuffing to tend to him. Instead, she settled for some instant soup and saltine crackers. Together, they spent an intimate, quiet day snuggled at home with just the company of Mickey Mouse and the Macy's Thanksgiving Day parade. That day would always be something special that he would cherish for life.

The early morning sounds of the city streets interrupted his reminiscent thoughts of Celeste. The heavy garbage truck's engine snuffed the fire engine's sirens in the background. Alvin could feel his stomach's cry for food but had to fight the urge. Especially for the next few hours. If he gave in to his desire to eat now it would stifle his work out routine. He heard Trevor making his way down the hallway toward the guest room, where he sat.

"You ready man?" Trevor asked knocking on the door.

"Yeah. I'm ready," Alvin responded picking up his leather gym bag. Trevor had already started down the steps by the time Alvin opened the bedroom door. He flipped off the bedroom light and made his way down the newly shellacked wooden stairs.

"Time to lose the fat and trim the excess,"

Trevor smiled pulling a .38 caliber gun out of the closet and tucking it inside his jacket.

"I see," Alvin replied raising an eyebrow.

"Don't you worry bout nothing mon. Every ting going to be smooth."

"I hope you're right, Trevor." *I truly hope you are,* Alvin thought.

"What's the name of the gym again?" Trevor asked opening the car door.

"Rough House man. Remember?" Alvin replied closing the passenger door once inside.

"Cool. Rough House it is then. And let's pray we won't have to define the name of that gym today."

"You mean to tell me no one knows where the hell he is? What about Tony? Have you found him yet?"

"Not yet, Mr. Gumichi. But we're on it round the clock," Nikko replied mildly.

Franchesco Gumichi, a well-built man, ran over to Nikko and punched him in the stomach. "Try harder. I want that punk Alvin here yesterday. I want that Benedict Arnold nephew of mine here now! Do I make myself understood?" Franchesco yelled storming out of the room and onto the balcony which overlooked the Chesapeake Bay. His black hair was slicked back in a pony tail which rested in the middle of his back and his thin mustache was the only distinguishing characteristic. Usually, Franchesco was a fairly reasonable man slow to anger. But this whole damn thing with Alvin and Tony disappearing with his stash and cash, had kept him on the wrong side of the bed.

He let out a deep breath and glared out over the balcony toward the Bay in deep thought. If only Alvin or his sister's son had called, had come to him before he had to seek them out, he would have understood, would have tried to work things out. Now, as it stood, there was only one thing he could do. The only thing left to do—and that was to set a permanent example.

Nikko rose up slowly from the floor. Franchesco's punch had wiped his breath out and leveled him to the floor. He brushed the pieces of carpet off his elbows then summoned two guys over to him.

"Look," he threatened pointing his finger in their faces. "It ain't that hard to find these punks. Find em! Today! If you find Tony, drag him here. If you find that other kid, beat him down till he gives up the packages, then rub him out. Put the word out on the streets. If he doesn't come in, we'll find a way to make him regret ever doing business with Mr. Gumichi. Also check the girlfriend's house again. Keep an eye on her. Maybe she'll lead us to the punk. Use whoever we must to get next to him!" Nikko waved the two burly men off then joined Franchesco on the balcony.

"Consider it done, Mr. Gumichi," Nikko assured.

"It better be. I can't afford not to find them.

I have too many people to answer to. You understand me, Nikko?" he squinted. "If I burn down, everybody is going down with me. You got that?"

"Yeah I got it boss. I got it," Nikko replied grudgingly. He excused himself and made his way back into the house. He had to find a way to rattle Alvin's spirit and quick, he determined. Because there was no way he was falling down with Franchesco. No way at all. Franchesco had too many connections and they all were within a hand's reach of snapping his neck. Nope, he couldn't go out of this world behind some greedy, careless, power-hungry kids. They would have to grab this kid Alvin now!

Twelve

The men's locker room was full considering the time of the day. Businessmen were taking advantage of the early hours at the Rough House gym. Alvin, drenched with sweat from his workout, sat on the wooden bench, waiting for the locker room to empty out. Trevor waited downstairs, ready to warn him if anyone suspicious came by. Alvin's eyes fixated on locker #918. He let the air seep through his nostrils slowly as he stared at his locker. From where he sat, everything looked normal. The padlock was still intact and the door still on the hinges. That was a good sign. A tall gentleman appeared suddenly in front of him. "There's a shower area available," the man motioned with his thumb.

"Thanks," Alvin said standing, deciding to head toward the shower. He could feel the man's eyes following him until he disappeared into the steam. *I'll sure be glad when this is all over. I can't feel safe anywhere. And I don't like having to look over my shoulder every minute,* Alvin protested quietly, stepping onto the cold, wet tile, waiting for the man to disappear.

* * *

Dante cruised the parking lot until he found a parking space near the back entrance. Backing into the parking space, he flickered his high beams at the blue van across from him. Their fog lights were on. The woman behind the wheel returned the signal by flashing her highbeams. Dante smiled and reclined his seat back slightly then adjusted the steering wheel. He grabbed the gym bag from the passenger seat and placed it on his lap.

God, I'm not up to this, he determined. He preferred to be home in his warm bed next to Celeste instead of sitting in the parking lot of the Rough House gym. Exercising always took a certain discipline that he had managed to develop. Until today. Things would be different today. Peeling back the paper to his Snicker's bar, he bit the candy in half. He would need something to get his blood jumping. And the sugar from the candy bar was just the thing, for now.

Nikko pulled into the gas station and parked the car in the corner next to the mutilated public pay phones and the two men standing near them. The men got into the black sedan with him.

Nikko didn't say a word. He spun off onto the streets, tires screeching, rubber burning.

"Mr. Gumichi wants some results within forty eight hours or else. That's the order sent down."

They spent the next thirty minutes scanning the inner city streets trying to find Alvin or anyone that would have information about his whereabouts. This whole shenanigan was starting to tick Nikko off. He gunned the engine through the yellow traffic light.

If Mr. Gumichi's stash wasn't recovered, there would be a lot of pissed off heads of the family and politicians. The disks offered vital information such as the names, addresses, social security numbers, birth dates, detailed physical characteristics, as well as a copy of several important fingerprints, which were cleverly lifted from wine glasses served at many of Franchesco's dinner parties. If he wanted to get information on a particular high-roller, he would invite him over to dinner, offer him some wine and lift his prints off the glasses when he was done. Franchesco had the state of the art technology and the people to run it. All Alvin and Tony were supposed to do was merge the data from Gumichi's disk to that of the FBI and DEA computer information. Franchesco wanted to see if there were any matches between the people he did business with and the FBI's informants and witness protection people. With this powerful information at his disposal, he could find out who was working both sides of the fence. It also gave him the opportunity to rub-out anyone who was straddling the fence. And with any luck, he would be able to penetrate the witness protection list and locate some of the pigeons that rolled over and kill them too. That's all those kids were assigned to do as a test of their loyalty. Franchesco should have never trusted them to make that delivery. But more important than that, Alvin and Tony should have never run off with the money and not delivered the merchandise. Never!

Just thinking about the deadly possibilities if this shipment was never retrieved, kicked Nikko into a frenzy. His heart began beating so fast that it was about to pop. Franchesco Gumichi meant business. He had laid down the order and he meant it done by yesterday. Nephew or not, these chumps were going for a long drive. Nikko smiled to himself. They are going down.

Alvin stepped out of the shower with a large, white, terry cloth towel wrapped around him. The locker room was empty except for the little, bald man sitting on the corner of the bench. His head hung low while he fumbled with his lock. Hearing Alvin's wet feet squashing across the floor, the little man looked up. "Morning," he mumbled.

"Morning," Alvin responded walking past him.

"You married?" the stranger asked unexpectedly.

"No," Alvin replied wryly. He really didn't want to engage this lonely man in conversation about marriage. There was no time. He had to get dressed, grab the bag out of the locker, meet Trevor downstairs and leave.

"Good. Don't ever get married. It'll break your heart one day. Believe me, it will."

Alvin didn't respond to the little man's apparent cry for help. After all, this wasn't his problem.

"Do you have kids?" the man asked moving closer to Alvin.

Alvin's panic light flew on. *Who the hell is this joker and what's his angle?* Alvin scowled inwardly then turned around slowly to face the man standing behind him. He had a picture of his family in one hand and a .45 magnum in the other. *This is it.* Alvin heeded. *Gumichi finally found me. Now what? Where the hell is Trevor and his metal machinery?* Alvin's head was spinning. He had to think of something quick before the bullet pierced his skin.

"Wait!" Alvin pleaded. "What's with the gun?"

"Oh this," the man said waving the gun around haphazardly. "It's my only true friend since my wife left me." He smiled wickedly. "Don't worry. I'm not going to do myself here."

"Come on man. Things can't ever be that bad where you feel like you have nothing to live for. Relax. Do you want to sit down and talk about it?" Alvin rationalized.

"Yeah? Well how about if there is something to die for? What about that Dr. Ruthie? Is there anything or anyone you'd be willing to die for?''

Alvin paused for a while reflecting on the stranger's question. Only Celeste.

"I didn't think so," the man said to Alvin's silence, tucking his gun in his waist. "You look like the kind who only cares about himself. Better watch yourself, mister, 'cause maybe somebody got it out for you too."

Alvin lay back against the lockers watching the little man stroll out of the room. He took a few deep breaths trying to retard his heart's fast momentum. Having his life flash before him, he was happy that he was still alive and it was just a glint. He had to get the hell out of here.

Trevor walked into the room just as Alvin finished tying his sneakers.

"What the hell you doing up here man? Let's go!" Trevor said motioning him with his hand.

"You don't want to know," Alvin replied wiping the sweat from his brow. "Let me get the bag with the disks and then we're out."

Trevor stood in the doorway to the locker-room glancing around for any signs of trouble. He had his hands in his pockets, where he had the .32 half cocked. "Hurry up mon. I'm getting an uneasy feeling about this."

Alvin peeked into the bag to make sure everything was still in place. Once he saw the two boxes of disks he zipped the bag back up, closed the locker and met Trevor in the doorway.

"Ready man. Let's roll," Alvin said patting his buddy on the back. "You got the keys to the car right?" he smiled.

"Right here," Trevor said swinging the keys.

Dante sat up when he noticed the black sedan backing in next to the blue van across from him. The guys in the car seemed a little bit north of their part of the hood as Dante's eyes locked with the large, white man sitting behind the wheel of the late model sedan. Who the heck were they and why were they hanging out in the parking lot on this side of town?

Just then, Alvin and Trevor appeared in the parking lot, both scanning the street and the lot for any negative signs. Dante spotted them first as he flicked his highbeams at the blue van. On cue, the woman behind the wheel of the van, dressed in aerobic gear, along with two men emerged from the van. They huddled together past Dante's car and gave him a quick glance. No sooner had they passed Dante than two men hopped out of the black sedan with their hands inside their jacket pockets.

What the hell? Dante mumbled jumping out of the car, drawing attention from the driver of the sedan. Stuff was about to get crazy and Dante wanted to grab Alvin before it did.

Trevor spotted the white men running towards them and yelled to Alvin, "Break mon!"

Alvin glared at the two familiar faces and ran

to the left. Trevor took off to the right, while the two men from the sedan and the three people from the van, raced after Alvin trailing slightly behind the two men from the sedan. Alvin was running wildly through the streets crashing into people and knocking them over.

Dante dragged behind the pack taking a shortcut up one of the alleys. After two blocks, one of the men from the blue van caught up to the two Neanderthals from the sedan. After tackling them to the ground, he stood over them with his gun pointing toward them. "Don't move," he scowled out of breath. "Or, I'll split your heads open."

Alvin had gained some distance between him and his other pursuers, so he thought. Glancing over his shoulder, he slowed up slightly when he noticed that the street he'd just run down seemed empty. But as soon as he turned his head around to face forward, he collided dead smack into Dante's chest causing them both to hit the hard pavement. Immediately after the impact, the woman and her other companion from the van stood over them both with their .357 Magnums drawn. "Cool it," the woman ordered pulling Dante off of Alvin. "Put your hands behind your head."

"What I do?" Alvin asked releasing the bag and placing his hands behind his head.

The woman handcuffed him and with the help of the other man, helped Alvin to the curb.

Dante stood in the background with a look of satisfaction sweeping across his face.

"What about him?" Alvin questioned pointing to Dante. "No one's going to haul his butt in?" he frowned.

"Watch your step," the woman advised pushing Alvin towards the two unmarked cars that had pulled alongside of them. Alvin was led to the second car, which was empty because the first car was occupied by the two men who had been wrestled down earlier on in the chase.

"Who the hell are you guys?" Alvin demanded, resisting entrance into the backseat of the car.

Dante walked over to Alvin and eased right up to his face and grinned. "FBI. Now get your sorry ass in the car."

Alvin's eyes lit up in shock. *Who? What? Why?* His mind stumbled over the questions as the car door slammed shut, causing him to jump.

"What about the other one, the driver?" Dante asked.

"He got away. Don't worry, we'll get that fat turd, too," the man reassured handing Dante Alvin's gym bag.

"Thanks," Dante said frustrated.

"Hey, relax," the woman smiled patting Dante on the shoulder. "Eventually, he'll spring up too and so will the rest of the gang. But for now, congratulations on a job well done KODY. We couldn't have gotten this far without your help."

Thirteen

"Nikko! What are you telling me?" Franchesco screamed into the telephone.

"I don't know what went wrong boss. We found him but I guess we weren't the only ones looking for him."

"Damn it Nikko! So what you're telling me is that the FBI has him?"

"The man who grabbed Johnny and Lou identified himself as FBI."

"Did that boy have the packages with him or not?"

"I don't know. I don't think so boss."

"Ah hell!" Franchesco yelled throwing the telephone into the wall then watching it break into three pieces. He would take care of Nikko later. Right now, he had to get his hands on those packages Alvin held before the Feds stormed his estate. More than likely, the Feds would ask Alvin a few questions and release him if he professed his innocence. Franchesco prayed silently that Alvin would keep his mouth shut and had stored the packages somewhere out of reach of the FBI.

If they released Alvin, he would have him

picked up immediately and brought to the house. But if they didn't let him go, that probably meant he was going to cut a deal and roll over. *I can't allow that to happen*, Franchesco vowed. He took another puff of his cigar then gulped down a shot of bourbon. The only way to guarantee that Alvin would keep his mouth sealed was to send a warning to him. Not just any kind of warning but one that would rock his life forever.

Iris and Tom pulled into the driveway in a white Lincoln Continental. NaNe and Celeste lingered on the front porch while Uncle Deak headed down the staircase to approach the car.

"Daddy," Iris grinned springing out of the car then hugging her dad as hard as she could.

"Hey baby girl," he grinned widely kissing her on the cheek. "You look good kiddo."

"Thank you, daddy. You don't look so bad yourself," she joked. "Come here daddy," she said tugging him over towards Tom. "I want you to meet Tom, my . . ." she hesitated.

"Pleased to meet you," Uncle Deak cut in extending his hand.

"Top of the morning to you too sir," Tom said in a heavy European accent, eyes shifting to the ground quickly.

Celeste walked to the edge of the porch while NaNe shadowed behind her.

"He's certainly not black. Nope, nowhere near it," NaNe mumbled nudging Celeste.

"What's wrong Little Bit? You look tired honey."

"I woke up this morning at 5:30 am and have been up ever since. I'm pooped NaNe."

"Really?" NaNe said backing away from her granddaughter then looking her over. "Something about Alvin?" she asked, panic-stricken.

"No. Don't worry, NaNe," Celeste said turning away to greet Iris with a smile as she made her way up the stairs. "We'll talk later," she whispered over her shoulder to NaNe.

"NaNe, Celeste," Iris beamed holding Tom's hand. "I want you to meet Tom. Tom, this is my aunt NaNe and my cousin Celeste."

"Welcome to Washington," NaNe said giving him an A-frame hug.

"Thank you," Tom grinned looking over NaNe's shoulder.

"Nice to meet you," Celeste chimed in giving him a warm handshake.

"Same here," Tom replied.

"Well, let's not stand here all day. Come on in and rest your feet," NaNe suggested holding the door open for everyone while she and Uncle Deak trailed behind.

Uncle Deak and NaNe followed Celeste, Iris and Tom into the trinket-filled livingroom, where they took a seat. NaNe asked everyone if they wanted something to drink while she kept her eyes glued on Tom. There was something about this character she didn't like. Besides the fact that he had shifty eyes.

Iris was the focus of attention as usual, as

she overpowered the conversations with her innocent smile and girl-like laugh. Celeste sank back into the worn sofa with her left elbow on the arm of the sofa and her fist pressed up on the side of her head. She was absorbing Iris' conversation with Tom's body language as the two held hands. Uncle Deak leaned forward in the Queen Anne chair, perhaps to get a better view of Tom and a closer observation of the enormous rock protruding from his daughter's finger.

The house was beginning to take on the familiar scent of NaNe's cooking. The aroma of fried bacon, homemade biscuits and hashbrowns crept past everyone's nostrils.

"Something smells good," Tom said sniffing continually to ingest more of the aroma.

"Yes it does. Let me find out just how long before we can eat," Uncle Deak said rising from his chair and walking into the kitchen.

There was a transitional moment of silence before Iris spoke first. "Celeste, where's Dante?"

"He had some other business to attend to today. But he told me to tell you and Tom that you must come over for dinner before you leave."

"Of course," Iris assured tapping Tom on the back of the hand. "Are you living over at his place permanently now?"

"Just for a little while longer. I should be back at my place soon."

There was another lull in the conversation

before Tom spoke up. "Celeste, Iris tells me
you have a convertible Mustang. I love con-
vertibles and I love Mustangs. Do you think
you could take us for a spin before we leave?"

"Sure. Better yet, I'll let Iris take Beauty and
the two of you can joy ride together if you
like."

"We'd love to! You hear that honey? Your
cousin is going to lend us her car."

"That's great darling. Thanks Celeste," Iris
smiled then winked at her cousin. "Celeste,
how am I ever going to tell daddy and NaNe
about me and Tom?" she whispered.

Tom stiffened up in his seat. Celeste
shrugged and replied, "There isn't going to
be a good time, cuz. All I know is the sooner
you tell them, the sooner it'll be over. And the
quicker Tom can stop looking so darn uncomfortable."

"But when should I tell them? Now? After
lunch? Tomorrow or what?" Iris huffed looking out the window. She looked uptight and
nervous to Celeste, which was rare for her
cousin who always possessed a great deal of
confidence.

"I don't know Iris. But I wish you'd be fast
about it because all this hush, hush stuff is
making my stomach knot."

Iris glanced over at Tom, whose eyes had
averted hers and were focusing on the tall ficus
plant in the corner. Tom's sudden stillness was
beginning to annoy Celeste. Why wasn't this
man helping her cousin with this family crisis?

How come he had no words of advice or ideas to share on the situation? Just as Celeste was about to address him, Tom shifted his eyes back to Iris and spouted, "I'll tell them."

"Tell who what?" NaNe said suddenly appearing in the living room with Uncle Deak standing behind her.

There was a rush of blood zooming through Celeste's, Iris's and Tom's veins as they all locked eyes, forming a triangle. Tom cleared his throat and rose up from his chair still clutching Iris's hand. Celeste shut her eyes momentarily then let out a long breath. The room stood motionless for what seemed like way too long. NaNe and Uncle Deak stood firmly awaiting an answer.

"So, what? The cat got everybody's tongue?" NaNe asked.

Celeste could see Tom's expression change from that of a happy, light look to that of an intense, negotiating stare. "Well," he started pulling Iris to her feet. "Iris and I have something else we'd like to share with you."

"Lord have mercy," NaNe cut in. "Don't tell me, Iris is pregnant." By now Uncle Deak had slid a little closer to Tom and Iris, anticipating Iris's response to NaNe's accusation. But Iris didn't budge. She was going to let her Prince Charming handle this one. At least, until things got a little haywire.

"No ma'am it's nothing along those lines. Nothing like that at all," Tom reassured.

"Then what is it, man? You're testing my patience," Uncle Deak replied, irritated.

Tom must have sensed uncle Deak's frustration because he finally got up enough guts to blurt out, "Your daughter and I got married."

Crash! Celeste heard her imaginary voice say. Stuff was about to get ugly, she imagined.

Instead, the atmosphere remained calm and soothing as uncle Deak strolled over to Tom and Iris and stood directly before them. He shook his head slightly then extended his right hand and softly replied, "Congratulations." Then he hugged Iris and cradled her back and forth as the tears rolled down his face. Iris held her father tightly then let her own tears escape down her cheeks as well. NaNe joined the circle by hugging Tom and Iris.

Celeste couldn't believe what was transpiring right before her eyes. NaNe and Uncle Deak seemed relieved and exalted all at once. She eventually made her way over to the newlyweds and embraced them both. She was surprised at how intrigued uncle Deak and NaNe were about Tom and his business and his marriage to Iris. Iris and Celeste grinned at each other in a pleasing manner. For the next few hours, Iris and Tom dazzled everyone with their first encounter story and tales that led up to their decision to marry. They apologized for not saying anything sooner but chucked it off as being an inevitable situation. NaNe and uncle Deak didn't seem to be the least bit perturbed about their secrecy. A good sign, Celeste thought. Perhaps they were learning how to let go and cut the umbilical cord as Iris would always say.

After lunch, Tom and Iris visited with the family for a while before deciding it was time to leave. NaNe headed to the kitchen and packed them some food to go. Uncle Deak chewed on Iris's and Tom's ears a little longer before Tom excused himself. "Pardon me Mr. Dunbar," he said pulling out his electronic organizer from his jacket. "I need to make a phone call. Is there a phone I can use . . . ?"

"Who you calling, darling?" Iris asked following Tom.

"I want to try and reach my cousin on my mother's side. You remember me telling you about him and how I haven't seen him in ten years. He's in Annapolis," he replied dialing the number.

"Oh yeah, that cousin. I guess you better call him, considering you've come all this way."

"Exactly," Tom said beginning to punch the numbers on the key pad. "By the way, is Annapolis considered long distance?"

"Don't worry about it," uncle Deak advised. "You're calling within the United States now. You don't have anything to worry about. Trust me."

Uncle Deak talked with Celeste and Iris while they waited on the porch for Tom to join them. Inside NaNe had finished wrapping the plates and was walking past the living room toward the front door when she saw Tom fumbling with the phone.

"What's the problem Tom?"

"The number that I'm trying to reach is disconnected."

"Did you try information? Perhaps they may have a listing."

"No. I'm afraid I don't know how to do that here yet."

"Here," NaNe instructed placing the bag down on the table and taking the phone away from him. NaNe dialed the information operator, waited for the voice to come on, handed Tom the phone, and headed for the front door.

Tom balanced the receiver on his shoulder then picked up the bag of food.

"What city sir?" the operator asked.

"Annapolis," Tom replied. "I need a number for Gumichi. Franchesco Gumichi."

Dante circled around Alvin, who was slouching in the metal chair puffing on a cigarette. The steel gray furnishings made the room glum and cold. *They should have cut some windows into the wall,* Alvin acknowledged quietly feeling claustrophobic from the lack of fresh air. He could feel Dante staring at him as if his gaze would pierce his skin. But Alvin remained calm and collected. If this brother wanted to know anything he was going to have to do more than stare at him.

"So how long you reckon I'll be sitting here?" Alvin said exhaling more smoke.

"As long as necessary," Dante fired back.

"What's your angle Dante? You plan on staring at me this whole time or telling me what the hell this is all about?"

"If you can't figure out what this is about then I'm afraid you could be sitting here all day," Dante said sitting down in the chair across from Alvin.

There was a brief moment of silence before Alvin mashed the cigarette butt in the ashtray. "What is it you want to know?"

Dante looked at Alvin then shook his head. "Let's start by talking about your affiliation with Franchesco Gumichi."

"Who?" Alvin said squinting.

"Listen you low life," Dante said jumping to his feet. "We can do it the easy way or the hard way. It's your choice. Frankly," he said leaning into Alvin's face, "it doesn't make me a bit of difference. Cause you see, I will be able to go home tonight to my warm, cozy bed next to my soft and cuddly woman."

Alvin flinched as his temper began to flare. He had to stay cool. Besides, he knew that Dante was tempting him, trying to incite some kind of emotional display. But he wasn't going to bite.

"I don't know," Dante said plopping down on the chair then putting his feet up on the long, rectangular desk. "Perhaps we should release you and call Franchesco and tell him you're on the streets. Maybe you'd prefer to talk to him." Dante took a deep breath then let it out. "Okay buddy. That's what we'll do," he said rising from his chair and walking over to the door. "I'll get somebody in here to give you a ride over to Annapolis."

Alvin stared down at the ashtray sitting on the desk. He had forgotten about Franchesco Gumichi and his bullies hunting him down. He knew if he was back out on the streets, it would be a matter of seconds before Gumichi and his boys picked him up. Given the way they had ruined his place and supposedly trashed Celeste's apartment, it was safe to assume they were beyond the talking and reasoning stages. Basically, his wings had been clipped, so to speak. There wasn't anything else he could do but embrace the extended hand of Celeste's new love. *What a jacked up situation to be in,* he thought. He wondered if Celeste had anything to do with him being apprehended by the FBI. Or, if she even knew that her new man was a part of the organization. *That son of a . . .* Alvin dismissed quietly. *How could he use Celeste like that just to get close to me? If this brother thought that he was going to keep his little secret hidden from Celeste, he was wrong. Because the first chance he got to spill the news to Celeste, he was going to do it.* However, he wasn't sure that he would ever have the chance. Not at the rate things were going. Playing his options over in his head once more, he knew his chances of staying alive for a while longer was to cooperate with Dante.

Clearing his throat as a signal that he wanted to squeal, Alvin called after Dante. "Hey," he said lowly.

Upon hearing Alvin's voice, Dante turned around mid way down the hallway and walked back toward the tiny interrogating room. "What can I do for you Mr. Brouchard?"

Alvin hung his head down, with his hands clasped together. He knew that once he gave up Gumichi, there would be no turning back. More than likely, he'd end up in one of those protection programs for the rest of his life. Away from the very city that he worshipped and the very woman that he now realized that he loved. What else could he do? What good would freedom be if he couldn't walk the streets of D.C. arm in arm with Celeste? He would be able to start over somewhere but where? He hated small, rural, mid-western cities whose population fell below 50,000 people. His mind was scattered all over the place trying to anticipate what would be next. Dante's voice shook him from his daze.

"So what's it going to be Alvin? Us or Franchesco Gumichi?"

"Me," Alvin replied sadly. "It's going to be me."

Alvin spent the rest of the afternoon explaining his relationship with Tony Lucero and Franchesco Gumichi to Dante and his cohorts while they held the mike to the tape recorder in his face.

They took a break twice. Once for Alvin to use the restroom and again for a quick sandwich and some juice. The questions were coming at him from all directions but he held up through them all. Finally, the question he had been anticipating all afternoon, came from Dante. He wanted Alvin to tell them what was on the diskettes. Alvin did one step better than that. For the promise of a protection program somewhere other than a mid-western city, Alvin offered to show them. In a matter of minutes, Dante and his co-workers had a computer system set up in the room. Everyone gathered around Alvin as he popped the diskette in the A drive. As the computer booted up Alvin let out a somber sigh. His life was definitely about to take on a different meaning. Even if he hadn't told the entire truth to Dante about the other packages.

Fourteen

Franchesco was waddling in the Jacuzzi thinking about Alvin and how the FBI had captured him. Feeling overwhelmed and tense about the events that had taken place, Franchesco needed to find a way to relax his mind. Besides, he had to get himself together before tomorrow night when he was scheduled to see Uncle Salvatore's son, his cousin, whom he hadn't seen in ten years. Nikko hadn't gotten any more word on Alvin or the whereabouts of the diskettes or the packages. It had been 24 hours since Alvin had been in the custody of the FBI. The way Franchesco saw it, Alvin must be considering turning over evidence, if he hadn't already. *No problem,* Franchesco mumbled to himself. He and Nikko had already set the warning sign in motion. After this little ordeal, Franchesco grinned wickedly, he was sure that Alvin would be too scared to say anything to anybody ever again.

"Hey beautiful," Dante greeted the voice on the other end of the phone.

"Where have you been, Dante?" Celeste asked switching the telephone to her other ear.

God help him. Dante didn't want to lie to Celeste but now was not the time to tell her the truth. He hadn't spoken to her or returned any of her messages in two days. How could he? He was too busy following up with this Alvin and Gumichi thing that he completely forgot about his personal life, something that always ended up being a problem for him in past relationships. Especially, when he chose to keep his identity as an agent confidential.

For the last three years he had served as an undercover, special agent for the FBI in the DC area. Although coaching was his true love, the job as a special agent was his true gig, allowing him to be a part of a challenging career that would make a difference in the area. Hearing Celeste clear her throat brought him back to the question at hand. He took a deep breath and lied, "I've been running around getting things settled so that we can have a fairly smooth basketball season."

"Really?" Celeste replied sarcastically. The phone fell dead again as Dante searched for the right words to say. He could tell by Celeste's aloofness that something was bothering her. He was sure it had something to do with his disappearing for the past two days. For the first time since the beginning of their relationship, Dante felt cornered. How was he going to explain to her that he really worked for the FBI out of the DC Branch and was using the coaching job as a means to disguise his true career? How would he tell her that he had been watching the organized crime ring in the D.C. area? What words could he whisper to make her understand that she would never see Alvin Brouchard again? Wanting desperately to wrap her in his arms, he blew out a tiny kiss over the telephone. "I'm sorry baby. I've been totally wrapped up in the events surrounding my life that I've neglected you for the past few days. Tell you what, let me make it up to you this weekend. I'll head over to NaNe's after I take a shower, pick you up and we can go over to the Baltimore Harbor for some shopping and a nice dinner. How does that sound?"

Celeste didn't answer right away. She was reflecting on how quickly Dante steered the conversation away from what he had been doing. Catching herself, she decided that she had too much going on with her studies to be preoccupied with Dante's comings and goings. Instead, she let out a soft laugh and said, "Dante, I don't appreciate not having my calls returned or my pages responded to. For two days I've been hanging out with Iris and Tom here at NaNe's wondering what was up."

"I know baby, I know. And I apologize for that. What do you say? Can we discuss this over dinner?"

"Uh hum I suppose I could use a little break and squeeze you in. Let me check my calendar and see."

"Oh, so now you've got to squeeze a brother

in huh? Sure hate to see what's going to happen to me once you set up your practice."

"You mean if you last that long. Cause I sure hate to see what's going to happen to you if you don't return my calls or pages in the future."

"Damn," he chuckled. "Cut a brother some slack darling. I said I'd make it up to you later baby," he cooed over the phone. "Guess what Celeste?"

"What," she said matter of fact-like.

"I'm about to step into the shower. I can wait till you get here if you want."

"I bet you could," she curtly replied. This whole thing with Dante's disappearing for two days and his roundabout answers made her skeptical. Not to mention the KODY thing a few days ago. Maybe if they spent some time together she would get some answers. Thinking about his proposal for a minute longer, she decided that she did want to see him and spend some time with him.

Celeste let out a sigh and replied, "Iris and Tom have my car because Tom wanted to take a spin in it before they left to head back to Europe. He left me that damn, huge, gangster looking Lincoln rental car. You know how I am about large cars. I can't stand them. I guess I'll have to pass on the shower, daddy."

"I love it when you talk to me like that baby. Maybe later then," Dante grinned.

"Maybe. It all depends."

"Well what time are they scheduled to come

back? Perhaps they'd like to join us for dinner."

"I don't think they'll be back in time. There was some talk about them sight-seeing the nation's capital and then going to French's Restaurant. Iris told Tom that now that he was in her neck of the woods, he had to eat some soul food," Celeste laughed.

"Well she's taking him to the right joint. Can't anybody do macaroni and cheese like Sharon French anyhow. Let me jump in the shower real quick and then I'll come and get you. Is NaNe home?"

"Why?"

"I just want to know if we'll have time for some loving that's all."

"Is that all you think about? Sex, sex, sex."

"No. Not always. Just when I'm near you or talking to you. That's the only time," Dante joked turning on the shower. "Let me go darling. I'll see you in a bit okay?"

"Okay. But don't take too long. NaNe is scheduled to come home in about two hours. See you when you get here big boy," Celeste teased hanging up the phone.

Dante smiled to himself. There was something about this woman that drove him crazy. Something about her talk, her walk, and her confidence that sent his head spinning. There had never been a woman like Celeste, who was able to grab his attention and hold it for as long as she did. He loved the way she hung right in there with him talking trash and giving him a hard time. As bizarre as it sounded, he needed a woman who would stand up to him and put him in check. Not even his best friend, Coach Johnson, or any of his players or co-workers got his adrenaline kicking like Celeste. Maybe, he would consider window shopping for a ring. Yup, that's about as close to a ring he would get. For now. Perhaps, if things kept zooming along the way they were for the next year, he'd present a ring to her next Christmas. What a way to bring in a New Year, he smiled as he let the hot water massage his skin.

Celeste stood in the mirror blow drying her hair. It had been a while since she had the spare time to go to the salon and have it done. She would have to find the time, she vowed looking into the bathroom mirror closer. She would wear something sensual, something loose this evening. Maybe her wrap dress with the side tie and deep V-neck cut and her matching gray suede high-heel pumps. It wasn't often that she was able to dress up in fine apparel and spend the night parading around town. Not since school started again. She felt as though something was going to happen tonight. She could feel it in her spirit. Perhaps all NaNe's lecturing and old-fashioned ways were starting to rub off on her. Regardless, she knew deep down that tonight something was about to change her life forever.

* * *

Iris and Tom pulled up at French's Restaurant just in enough time to grab the parking space in front of the frequented soul food restaurant. Iris parallel parked Beauty in between two larger vehicles. Thank God the Mustang was a small car because Iris was sure if Beauty had been a few feet longer, she would have never been able to fit into the parking space.

The restaurant was crowded as usual with the after work crowd beginning to pour in. The line started as soon as they walked in the door. Tom scanned the restaurant looking for somewhere for them to sit. "I see a table by the window. Do you want to claim it while I place the order?"

"Gladly," Iris said walking toward the table and placing her jacket around one of the chairs. She walked back over to Tom, excusing herself as she made her way toward the middle of the line. "I'm going to have macaroni and cheese, fried chicken, greens and corn bread."

Tom gave her an uncertain look as if he had never heard the words before. Iris laughed recognizing for the first time their cultural differences.

"What are greens?" Tom whispered to Iris.

"They're a leaf vegetable. Try them Tom. They're good."

"And what else am I supposed to eat with them? Come on, honey," Tom said at Iris' annoyed look. "I just have never eaten any of this food that's all," he said grabbing two trays. "Be patient with me Iris. After all, I was patient with you when you met my family and grimaced at the five course Italian spread my mama prepared."

"You're right sweetheart. That's true. Do you have a taste for chicken or red meat?"

"Preferably red meat. How about those right there?" he asked pointing to the ribs. "Let me try those."

"The ribs?"

"Is that what they're called?"

"Yes."

"Okay. Then I'll have the ribs and those green things you were telling me about and some of the bread you ordered. What's it called again?"

"Cornbread," she said, somewhat embarrassed as the person behind the register stared at Tom in bewilderment.

"Yeah well, that too," he smiled searching for his wallet. "I can't find my wallet Iris. I think I gave it to you back at the museum. Would you be a dear and please check your purse."

"I left it under the seat of the car. I'll be right back," she said jogging toward the front door.

The people behind them in line were starting to get restless, waiting for them to settle their bill. But Tom humored them by turning around and saying, "That's tourists for you." A few people snickered as Tom left his place in line, along with the food to see what was taking Iris so long.

Iris had trouble turning the key to the car door lock. Something Beauty always gave her trouble with. This car was so darn particular and fussy that she was sure Beauty only liked for Celeste to drive her. The cars were speeding past her so fast that she could feel her body being shaken by the pressure. All the more reason for her to get this damn door open before that truck came any closer, she thought tugging on the key. Looking up at the last minute she could see the headlights of the large truck moving closer. "My God Beauty," she said aloud. "Come on and open up for dear old cousin Iris won't you." The truck's engine was revving louder as it approached her. The evening sun had set which made it more difficult for her to see what she was doing. Why in God's name didn't she put her purse under the passenger's seat? Better yet why hadn't she tried to enter on the passengers's side, she thought just as the truck whizzed next by her.

Iris knew something was terribly wrong when she hit the ground. "Oh God," she screamed as the force and speed of the truck sucked her under its back wheels. The squeal of Iris' voice along with the thump of her body being rolled over caused everyone to run out of the restaurant.

"Oh Lord," Tom cried out loud. "Iris, Iris," he screamed running behind the truck. The truck had come to a stop midway down the block. "Somebody get help! Please!" Tom yelled.

A passerby in a jeep jumped out of the car and ran over to the truck, where Tom and the driver knelt down next to Iris's mangled body. Her legs lay crumpled and wedged beneath the wheels of the truck. No one could see Iris's face. Blood was everywhere and the scene gruesome.

The paramedics, firefighters and police officers had arrived in less than five minutes and cleared the mounting crowd. Tom was having some kind of breathing attack when somebody pulled him away from the scene and began administering oxygen to him. The firefighters and paramedics fought quickly and diligently trying to free Iris from under the truck, hoping and praying that she would fight hard to hold on. One hour later they were finally able to free Iris from the snare of the truck. As the paramedics carefully pulled her limp body from under the truck, they knew right away that she didn't have a chance. Iris had fought for as long as she could but the truck wheels had defeated her. Iris' life had been snatched away.

Dante had picked Celeste up forty-five minutes after their conversation. His intentions were to slide in a quick one, which really wouldn't be all that quick, before NaNe returned. But by the time he reached the little brownstone, NaNe along with two of her church friends had returned. Naturally the house smelled of fried fish, gravy, biscuits and grits, as this was to serve as NaNe's and her guests' dinner entree. NaNe offered for them to stay, but Dante politely refused, stating that he had made plans for him and Celeste for the evening. Glancing over at Celeste, he could feel his excitement lingering in the pit of his stomach. His heart was at ease knowing that Alvin and his indiscretions would no longer pose a threat to his sweetheart. Celeste was busy staring out the window and grooving to the sounds of Gerald Albright and hadn't noticed Dante's occasional glimpses. She had the dozen long-stemmed white roses he had lavished upon her at NaNe's front door laid across her lap.

"Why don't you lay them across the back seat, sweetie?"

Celeste turned away from the bustle of the busy streets, looked at Dante and replied, "They feel good right where they are. I should have put them in a vase at NaNe's but I guess I didn't want to part with them."

Dante grinned and swept Celeste's left hand up with his right hand. Holding it ever so gingerly, he caressed her hand. "Celeste, I have so much I want to say to you," he said pulling into the circular driveway at the Hyatt hotel.

"I thought we were going to dinner Dante?"

"We are darling. But I thought we'd make a night of it so I got us a suite. Just you and me tonight. No family members, no telephone calls, no pagers beeping," he said opening the glove compartment and tucking the pager inside. "Just the two of us, we can make it if we try," he sang leaning over and kissing her on her neck. "Where's your jacket baby? It feels a little bit nippy for forty-five degrees."

"It's on the back seat," she grinned. "So, this is our night together, right? No early morning wake-up calls, no last minute business to attend to. Just me and you, is that correct?"

"Correct sweetheart. Just me and you."

The bellman opened the door for Celeste and helped her out of the car sneaking a peek at her legs. Dante got a package out of the trunk before handing the parking attendant his keys.

"This should do it," he said, holding the hotel door open for Celeste.

Celeste nestled down in the large, Paris, leather armchair while Dante went to check them in. The lobby of the hotel was magnificent with large urns filled with dried flowers, plenty of soft oversized chairs in an array of soft, neutral colors and several neo-classical paintings hung about. Watching Dante's confident strides as he made his way over to her, made her heart skip. Dante was certainly as fine as they came by Celeste's definition. Every time he dressed up he exuded a smoother, richer look. He had on a tan and green plaid jacket with a thin burgundy pinstripe outlining the colors. Underneath the jacket, neatly tucked in his tan, baggy slacks, was a ribbed burgundy crew neck shirt. To top off the ensemble he had on a pair of tan, burgundy and green designer socks which emphasized his burgundy, tasseled, Italian-cut leather shoes. His gold watch was the final item that touched off the outfit. Nothing about Dante was cheap, not even his cologne.

Celeste felt proud to be with a handsome, well-groomed gentleman as they strolled toward the elevators arm in arm. The inside of the elevator was decorated with glass and dark, rich wood throughout. Dante hit the button marked seventeen, waited for the elevator doors to close then reeled Celeste into his chest.

"I've missed you," he said softly biting the back of her neck.

"I've missed you too. What have you been doing to keep your mind so full?"

"Thinking about you and how I don't ever want to lose you."

"Really?" she said looking up at him curiously.

"Truly sweetheart," he said kissing her on the nose. "I love you so much Celeste. Can't you feel how strong it is? I feel like God made you especially for me."

"I love you too, Dante. I just hope," she paused catching herself. It was not the time to talk about his past or his career.

"What?" he said seriously. "What were you about to say?"

"Nothing. I think what I was about to do was dampen the evening," she smiled broadly.

"I don't think you could even if you tried. This is our stop," he said holding the elevator doors open long enough for Celeste to step out. The lobby was lined with a thick, plush red carpet. The cherry wood server table sat on the left side of the lobby with an oval mirror above it. Walking past the mirror, Dante stopped suddenly, held Celeste then gazed into the mirror. He had his arms around her waist and his chin on her shoulder as she faced the mirror with him.

"What a great looking couple," he said taking a moment to capture the view. "I think we'll have some beautiful children if they get their looks from their mother."

"I think they'll earn their looks from their dad."

"How about from us both? We'll have a little girl that looks like you, a little hard headed boy, who will favor me, and a surprise baby, who will take on both our attributes. What do you think?"

"I think three children is a bit much. How about one child with both our characteristics?"

"One child? Come on baby," he said turning her around to face him. "Can we at least meet somewhere in the middle and have two?"

"I'll think about it," she said kissing him on the lips. An elderly gentleman stepped out of his room just as Dante returned Celeste's kiss.

"Good evening," he grinned making his way around them.

"Good evening," they giggled and walked down to their room.

"Should I carry you across the threshold?" Dante said slipping the card in the slot then opening the door.

"Sure you can carry me," Celeste said entering the room. "When it's time for you to." She winked then turned and walked into the suite.

The room was lavishly furnished with 18th century pieces. Unique vases filled with exotic flowers were cleverly scattered about the room. The dark, thick drapes were left partly open, allowing the view of the harbor. Celeste stood staring out the large window enjoying the picturesque sight. Although she appreciated Dante's efforts, something still didn't quite feel right. Maybe it was her deep, inner voice that made her feel that all this was a bit much for someone that wasn't on their honeymoon. She took a seat on the thick sofa. She was exhausted playing house with the brothers and never lasting long enough to make the dream come to life. Playing patty-cake with Alvin for two years had tainted her view of relationships and the investment of time that they required.

"What are you thinking about darling?" Dante asked sliding next to her and slipping his arm around her shoulder.

"Us," she said letting out a soundless sigh. "I just don't want us to get stuck," she whispered turning to face Dante.

"What do you mean?" his face getting tight suddenly.

"You know," she shrugged her shoulders. "Like playing at love yet not really wanting it bad enough to keep it. Being able to make a commitment." Visions of Alvin played in her mind.

Dante studied her face for a long while as if he were painting a picture. He seared her facial characteristics into his memory, focusing on all her features. He cracked a faint smile as he reflected on a game that he once played with a group of friends when he was dating his ex-girlfriend Denise. In the game, the men were blind-folded, turned around a few times and led to the sofa where one of the women sat. The idea of the game was to be able to feel the hands and face of the woman and decide if she was your girlfriend. He would never forget that day. At least, while he lived with Denise, she wouldn't let him. Mainly because when it came to his turn to decide if the woman on the sofa was his girlfriend, he failed. Now looking back, he knew why. He truly didn't know the meaning of love and its power until he laid eyes on Celeste. He was sure of one thing. If he ever had to play that game again, he would undoubtedly know Celeste.

Dante's eyes searched Celeste's face as he ran his hand through her hair. Gently, he pulled her head forward until it touched his forehead. Their eyes passionately clicked together for a few seconds before Dante finally replied, "I love you Celeste. You are everything I would want in a woman. Believe me when I tell you this is not some kind of game or pit stop for me. If you only knew how much I loved you, we wouldn't be having this conversation. But I want to set your heart at ease so listen to me closely." He paused moving his head up and down in an affirmative gesture until she mimicked the same motion.

"Are you listening?" She shook her head yes and he continued. "There is nothing I wouldn't do for you. Nothing. I love you so hard and so deep woman that I would die for you. I mean this from the depths of my heart," he said pressing his left hand against his heart as if he was pledging allegiance.

The words brought thin streaks of tears down Celeste's face. All of her life, she would visualize some special man in her life uttering similar words of love, of sincerity. She could hear the wind wrestling the water against the boats docked at the harbor. Dante kissed her tears away as he softly mumbled, "I love you Celeste."

Celeste could not respond to Dante's comments. The moment was too intense, too special to ruin by speaking. Instead, she let her body collapse to Dante's wet, caressing kisses.

"Just hold me Dante," she said softly. "I don't want this night to escape us so quickly."

"Okay darling," he said kissing her forehead as he had done so many times over the last few months. "I don't want it to pass by too quickly either."

Music filled the room as Celeste and Dante lay silently knitted in each other's arms. Celeste smiled widely as she absorbed Stephanie Mills' lyrics wondering if the song was specifically written for her because she certainly felt good all over. They lay in the midst of the soft moonlight shining through the large window, cherishing the moment. The connection between them had grown stronger over the months. Softly Dante whispered, "If anything ever happened to you, I don't know what I would do."

"Don't worry, Dante. Nothing is going to happen to me. We've got a good thing going here. Nothing is going to jeopardize that okay?" she gleamed kissing his hand.

Dante hoped she was right. He didn't know how long he could keep his true identity hidden from her. In fact, he wasn't sure how she would react to hearing that he was indeed somebody other than plain old Assistant Coach Lattimore. Perhaps this would be the time to share with her his real career. Now would be his chance to explain to Celeste that his decision to become an FBI agent was largely due to his dad, rest his soul, Clive Lattimore. He had been a military man turned CIA agent after serving as an officer in the Air Force for twenty years.

At first, Dante wasn't that comfortable with following his father's footsteps. In fact, Dante was very adamant about becoming a professional athlete. When the professional recruits had not chosen him upon his graduation from college, he was forced to do some soul-searching. After a few uneventful years in corporate America, Dante decided to apply for the FBI position. Simultaneously, he was offered the position of Assistant Coach for the small college basketball team in the DC area.

Snapping out of his trance, Dante squeezed Celeste tighter. Maybe if he told her now, when things were so calm and still, her reaction might be normal, understanding even. He worked through everything in his mind. He would have to tell her that Alvin was out of their lives for good, that she would never be able to lay eyes on him again or hear his voice thanks to Special Agent KODY. He had worked so hard to get this close to her, to penetrate her guarded wall while protecting her, that he didn't want to shatter it all with one confession. No, he continued thinking silently, he would wait until another time. A more practical time, a less romantic time. Probably tomorrow he would tell her the truth.

The night crept by with Celeste waking up in the king-size bed nestled in Dante's arms. Her head lay in the middle of his hairy chest with her silk slip exposing her left thigh, which was intertwined with Dante's left leg. Celeste whispered, "I love you" in Dante's ear, while she watched him sleep. *He must be exhausted*, Celeste thought quietly listening to his breathing which was light and steady. His eyes were cracked faintly and his mouth partly open when she placed a light kiss on his lips, slid out of bed into the bathroom where she filled the large Jacuzzi. It had been ages since she'd engulfed her body in the soothing ripples of a bubble bath. Celeste sprinkled a few bubble beads under the gushing water until the water foamed up. Once the tub was three quarters of the way full, Celeste slid into the warm water and let out a sigh. How long had it been since her last bath, she wondered leaning her head back against the cool tile. Closing her eyes, she began counting her breaths, slowly exhaling until her body was completely relaxed. She concentrated on calm, pretty things as she reaffirmed in her head how grateful she was to be alive and healthy. Inaudibly, she praised God and tried to seek His face, feel His presence, as her body fell numb to the warm water. *Thank You, Thank You,* she sang over and over in her head breathing heavier each time.

Thirty minutes or so later, she opened her eyes to find Dante standing before her naked. "Good morning," he smiled crouching down beside her. "Mind if I join you or is this a private session?" Celeste hesitated for a minute, wanting desperately to say that it was a private moment but that the session was over.

"I don't mind," she said leaning forward to make room for his tall body. Dante descended down into the water, shaking slightly once his body was immersed. "It's a little chilly in here," he shuttered through clamped teeth.

"I can run some more hot water if you'd like," she said cupping the water over his exposed knees.

"That's okay, sweetheart. I'll be fine. Just being next to you gives me the chills," he chuckled.

"Is that right?"

"That's correct, precious. What were you in here dreaming about, if you don't mind me asking?"

"Nothing in particular. I guess I was just doing some thinking."

"Oh yeah? What about?" he asked rubbing the bar of soap across her back.

"I don't know Dante, I need to remember my goals and do my best to keep on the straight and narrow. It's a continuous spiritual battle that I go through from time to time you know?" she said glancing at him over her shoulder.

Dante knew exactly what Celeste was battling with and it had a lot to do with him. Ever since the break in at her apartment a month ago, Celeste had been hinting around to getting back to her own space. He couldn't much blame her considering she had gotten into a routine, a rhythm with a man she had only known for five months. After living with Alvin and investing so much time in their relationship, Celeste was not thrilled to be in another live-in situation no matter how temporary it seemed. Perhaps it was time for her to get settled back in her own home. Now that Alvin and his conspiring cohorts no longer posed a threat, he would suggest that she move back to her place whenever she wanted.

"I know what this is about Celeste," Dante said rinsing the soap off her back. "You're ready to move back to your place, aren't you?"

She laughed, shook her head and replied, "I thought we agreed that you would stop reading my thoughts." Celeste blew the statement off as a joke when in fact it was clear that she and Dante had a special connection, a spiritual bond.

"I told you, baby girl, there's no such thing. Now let's get up from here," he said standing with water dripping from his body, "and get back to the house so we can get you moved back to building J."

He stepped out of the tub and gave Celeste his hand to help her out. He could feel his nature starting to lift as he observed Celeste's body and all its magnificent curves. Celeste noticed it too but chose to drape a towel around her body then handed him a similar white, terry cloth towel to do the same. Dante followed her lead because it was apparent that she was not pressed to be intimate today no more than she was last evening. This was fine with Dante because he would respect her decision no matter what the sacrifice. The way he figured, he had sampled the fruit, knew what it tasted like and was perfectly willing to wait for the next serving. No matter how long it took.

Fifteen

When Celeste and Dante turned onto NaNe's block, their eyes were immediately drawn to NaNe's driveway. There were several cars crammed in the driveway and a few more aligning the curb in front of NaNe's house. From what Celeste could tell, Uncle Deak, Aunt Ruthie and a few more relatives were visiting NaNe. How much could have happened in twenty-four hours? Celeste thought as her suspicions rose.

"I wonder what's going on?" Celeste murmured looking over at Dante.

"Beats me," Dante shrugged.

"NaNe didn't mention anything about a family dinner. I hope everything is all right," she said in a serious tone stepping out of the car. Dante met her on her side of the car and they began walking up the stairs leading to the front porch. The room fell completely silent when Celeste and Dante entered into the foyer. For the first time ever, the atmosphere at NaNe's house felt somber, chilly and cold. Everyone looked like they had been awake all night. Celeste quickly scanned the room searching for NaNe.

"Hello," Celeste said hesitantly. "Where's NaNe?"

"She's upstairs lying down," Aunt Ruthie said guiding her by the elbow. "Have a seat sugar," she continued practically pushing Celeste down in the oversized chair. Dante immediately followed her and took his place beside her. He could feel something in his gut as soon as he walked up the front stairs that something was wrong.

"What's wrong?" Celeste asked with an edge in her voice.

Aunt Ruthie glanced at Cousin Charlotte, who passed her gaze to Uncle Sammie, who in turn raised his eyebrows at Uncle Deak.

Uncle Deak hobbled over to Celeste, clasped her hands and murmured, "It's your Cousin Iris," he paused trying to fight back the tears welling up in his eyes again. Celeste's heart was thumping louder and faster now. She barely heard her own voice over her heartbeat, which was now ringing in her ears.

"What about Iris, Uncle Deak?" her eyes wide and concerned.

Uncle Deak took a moment to clear his throat and fight back the lump that was rising in his esophagus. "There's been an accident. A terrible, terrible accident," he said shaking his head continuously while the tears streamed down his face. "Little Bit, Iris is gone. She's, she's . . ." He couldn't finish the sentence. Instead, he broke down and began crying out of control. Uncle Sammie reached for him first, pulling him to his feet and leading him to the sofa.

The room went still, blurry like someone had dunked Celeste's head under water then tried to talk to her while she was still under. Her mind fumbled through his words as she shook her head savagely in disagreement. "No, no. I didn't hear what you said Uncle Deak," she said, eyes pleading with Aunt Ruthie. "Accident? Aunt Ruthie, what hospital is Iris in?"

"Celeste," Aunt Ruthie said calmly while cupping her hands over her forehead. She took a deep breath and knelt down next to Celeste. "Sweetheart, Iris is gone. There's been an accident. They tried to save her but they couldn't. I'm sorry, honey, she's gone."

"Gone where? Where did she and Tom go? What kind of accident?" Celeste shouted, her voice rising in pitch. She was hysterical, crying and squealing all at once.

Dante closed his eyes and bit his bottom lip. This was not happening, he prayed quietly. *Please Lord don't let this be happening*, he pleaded. But when he opened his eyes he knew it was real. Iris was dead.

After helping Cousin Charlotte calm Celeste down, Dante went upstairs to check on NaNe. NaNe didn't respond to the tap on the door so Dante entered the room anyway. Slowly he walked over to NaNe's bed, where she lay asleep with her Bible tucked in her bosom. He turned off the little lamp that was shining in NaNe's face and left the room. Then it hit him. He wondered where Tom was and how he was handling Iris' accident. Dante searched the entire house before he spotted Tom sitting in the back yard on the picnic bench with his head down on the table.

Dante's unexpected touch startled Tom as he jumped up off the seat. He let out a sigh of relief when he noticed that it was Dante.

"Are you okay, Tom?" Dante said feeling somewhat stupid for asking the question but he didn't know what else to say.

"No," he whispered letting the tears stream down his face.

Dante kept silent figuring it would be the best thing since he had no idea how to help Tom during this traumatic time. All Dante could remember from when his father died was wanting to be left alone. Perhaps that would be best, he resolved, standing up to head back to the house.

"I should have gone out there myself," Tom mumbled. "I should have never let her go."

Dante sat back down next to him folding his hands together. "Let her go where, Tom?"

Tom looked at Dante wondering if he would hold him responsible for having let her go back to the car. "Out to the car," he blurted. "Out to the damn car. I should have gone," he cried shaking his head in disbelief.

"Why? What happened?"

"I left my wallet, she went to get it and that's when it all happened," he muttered.

"When what happened?" Dante pushed a little more.

"When the truck came by and took her away. Oh my God," he whimpered harder. "I vowed to take care of her. I said I would never let anything happen to her. Never!"

Tom had completely lost control again and cried desperately. Dante did the best he could to console him by placing a light touch on his shoulder. He wanted desperately to ask Tom more questions but realized that would be impossible given his present state. For a minute, he imagined how he would have reacted if it had been Celeste. He felt the tears begin to rise up in his eyes and fought hard to suppress them.

Dante assisted Tom back into the house and brought him a bowl of hot soup that Aunt Ruthie had brewing on the stove.

"Keep an eye on him for awhile," he whispered to Aunt Ruthie. "I'm going to check on Celeste and NaNe."

Aunt Ruthie stopped him by placing her hand on his forearm. "They're both resting. NaNe is still resting upstairs and Celeste is relaxing on the sofa. Let them rest some more. Would you like some soup?"

"No thanks," Dante said plopping down at the kitchen table across from Tom. All the drama had caused him to lose his appetite. He fixed his gaze on Tom trying to fit the pieces of the puzzle together when Tom broke his silence. "They said the truck driver was drunk. That's why he didn't see Iris initially."

"Who's that?"

"The policemen who arrested the drunken bastard. They said he was over the damn legal limit. If you ask me," Tom paused looking at Dante with daggers in his eyes, "I think they shouldn't even have a limit in this country. Why even bother? Why even encourage people to do it in the first place? Then tell them if they do drink, they can only have X amount depending on your age and weight. I ask you good man, what kind of system is that?"

Dante didn't reply as Tom pushed away from the table, strolled over to the patio and stared sightlessly out the large glass door. If only he could do it over again. He heard Celeste's voice behind him and turned slowly to face her. Upon seeing her face, the tears began to roll down his cheeks again. The resemblance between her and Iris was strong. She gave him a faint smile, which he managed to reciprocate in the midst of his sadness.

Celeste grabbed Tom by the hand then fell into his embrace. She fought to maintain control, swallowing hard to keep the lump from surfacing again. No words were exchanged for several minutes as the two grieved for Iris the best way they knew how.

Dante had a chance to go upstairs and peek in on NaNe. Knocking on the door softly, the voice on the other side invited him in.

"Come on in," NaNe said in a husky voice and looked up at the doorway.

"It's me Mrs. Dunbar," Dante whispered upon entering the room. "How are you feeling? Do you need anything?"

"Yes," she said pausing to look up at the ceiling. "I need some answers. I don't understand how this happened. Do you?" she said pushing herself up in the bed. "I have buried too many people in my lifetime, Dante. I just can't take it anymore. At the rate things are going, there'll be no one left to bury me," she said shaking her head. "I just can't do it no more. You hear me. No more!" she cried.

Dante sat on the bed beside her and held her hand. "I know NaNe." He let her work through her emotions, weeping, whining, wondering, while he held steadfast to her hand.

"Dante, promise me you'll look after my baby," her eyes pleading with his.

"I will NaNe. I promise."

"Don't let her go anywhere without you by her side, okay?"

Dante couldn't answer right away. The promise was too difficult to keep. How was he supposed to shadow Celeste and her every move? He hung his head low trying to contemplate an acceptable answer for NaNe. After thinking about it for a moment, he shook his head in agreement.

"NaNe, I will do my very best to protect your granddaughter. And I will pray very hard that God sees to it that I will with His help."

NaNe let a tiny smile creep across her face showing approval. "Thank you son," she said patting his hand. "Thank you." Just as the atmosphere in the small antique room was starting to feel cheery, NaNe suddenly gripped her chest with her left hand and bowed forward grimacing from obvious pain.

"What's wrong NaNe?" Dante said jumping up off the bed.

"My heart Dante," she choked off her sentence slightly. "My blood pressure done shot up. Get me my pills there," she ordered pointing over to the dresser. Dante darted across the room, snatched the pills off the dresser and brought them back over to her. He snapped the lid off and dumped several tablets in his hand then held it out for her to take them.

Quickly, she gulped two tablets down without water handing Dante the glass on her table.

"Please," she said faintly still holding her heart.

He ran over to the bathroom, filled the glass with water and returned to the room with the full glass and water dripping from his hands.

"Here you go," he said holding the glass to her mouth while she sipped the water down.

"That was a close one. Thank you," NaNe smiled leaning back against the pillow. "The pain will subside shortly. Come here, Dante," she said in a heavy breath and patting the side of her bed.

Dante obliged the request and sat back

down on the bed. NaNe studied his face momentarily as if she was trying to enter his brain. She waited until the short breaths relaxed then she continued. "Do you love my granddaughter?"

Without blinking an eye and with total poise, Dante responded, "Yes ma'am. With all my heart and soul."

She searched his face some more looking for something deeper. "What are your intentions, dear?"

"To take care of Celeste. To be there for her whenever she needs me and whenever she thinks she doesn't. To make her my wife and the mother of my children if she so chooses."

"I believe you. From the first time Celeste brought you over here, I knew you were sincere. It's a feeling I had. A discerning of the spirit if you will. But let me ask you one more thing and I promise I'll quit leaning on you. Is there anything you have in your past that could hurt my granddaughter?"

Dante's body language told it all when he shifted positions and looked away from NaNe. NaNe's eyes stayed focused on him. Patiently she waited for Dante's response. Something about his sudden change in posture told her that indeed he had something to hide. Silence hung in the room temporarily while Dante scanned his brain for the right answer, a favorable reply.

"There is nothing in my past or future that would hurt Celeste. Only protect her. That's the best I can tell you NaNe. Honestly, that's the only thing I can say for now."

"Uh hum," NaNe said giving him a leveled look. She processed his response and decided to let it lie. For some reason she could not explain, she knew that it was better to leave this bit of his business alone.

Celeste searched the three rooms downstairs before making her way up the narrow, spiral staircase. She wanted to tell Dante about her conversation with Tom. Tom was headed to Annapolis to see a cousin he hadn't seen in ten years. He had no idea his cousin was the notorious crime boss, Franchesco Gumichi.

"There you are," Celeste said joining NaNe and Dante in the bedroom. "I was wondering where you were," she fretted placing a kiss on his cheek and then one on NaNe's.

"How are you feeling NaNe?"

"Devastated. I just can't believe it," NaNe glumly replied. "How's Deak holding up? Is he alright? Maybe I should go downstairs and look in on him," she said getting up off the bed. "I'll be downstairs if you need me," her voice trailed off as she headed down the hallway.

Celeste was glad that NaNe left the room because the sadness was starting to creep through again. And she really didn't have any energy left to cry again.

"How are you doing?" Dante said cuddling Celeste in his chest. "My baby holding up?"

Celeste shrugged and said, "I suppose so,"

then smiled weakly. "Dante you're never going to believe what I just learned. Remember, I told you that Tom wanted to take Beauty for a joy ride?"

"Yeah," Dante replied with a puzzled look.

"Do you know where they were trying to go but instead chose to stay in the D.C. area?"

"No."

"Annapolis."

"Yeah, and," Dante paused waving his hand for her to get on with it.

"Who lives in Annapolis, Dante?"

"Celeste you're not making any sense. What are you trying to say? Thousands of people live in Annapolis. So?"

"So, how many of them are reputed crime lords?"

Dante's face grew weary. He was too exhausted to play the cat and mouse game with Celeste.

Celeste watched Dante's face hoping that the clue would ring a bell. But no such luck. This brother's mind was out for the evening.

Celeste huffed then flicked her tongue against the back of her teeth, irritated that Dante couldn't or wouldn't make the connection. She waited as long as she could before blurting out, "Franchesco Gumichi."

"What?" Dante said moving so abruptly that it threw Celeste off balance. "Franchesco Gumichi? Why would Tom go see him? I mean, how does he know him?"

"Franchesco is his cousin, a first cousin that

he hasn't seen or talked to in several years. Can you believe that? He and Iris were supposed to meet him at his house in Annapolis before they went back to Europe." Celeste's face suddenly turned cold as she realized she would never see her cousin again. Never be able to share another conversation about men, relationships or just plain talk with her again. Dante sensed her thoughts and swiftly wrapped his arms around her again.

"Does Tom have any idea the kind of man Franchesco is?"

"I don't think so. He barely remembers what he looks like let alone what he does. I hope Tom will be okay. This is so hard on him. You know?"

"Yeah I know sweetheart," Dante said warmly. Lord forgive him, he asked quietly, but he wasn't thinking about Tom at this moment. He was more concerned with the notion that Tom and Franchesco were relatives. And how there would be a good possibility that Franchesco would show his respects by attending the memorial service. *Good God*, he frowned inwardly, *this is too close for anyone's sake. Iris' husband is related to Franchesco?* The next set of thoughts sent a wave of nausea over Dante. *What if Iris' accident wasn't one after all? What if the driver mistook Iris for Celeste? What if Tom has been a part of this whole scheme?*

Dante's head was spinning like someone had swung him around for two minutes then let him go. He had to get some air and sort this stuff out fast. *Would now be a good time to tell Celeste the truth about his identity?* he wondered. *Probably not,* he resolved. He didn't want to burden Celeste with any more surprising news and he certainly didn't want her worrying unnecessarily. Dante shut his eyes tightly then leaned his head back toward the ceiling. *Damn this is crazy,* his mind screamed quietly. He decided to say nothing until he had investigated the matter further. *The first thing to do?* he determined internally, *was to start with the driver of the delivery truck. Then try to get some information on Tom Santini.*

Sixteen

Dante bent down and swiped his vacationing neighbors' newspaper after he returned from his morning jog. The past few days had been stressful on everyone, especially Celeste. The preparation for the funeral services was taking its toll on the entire family. And Dante was partly relieved that the funeral was today. All the bickering and arguing by the Dunbar clan, about trivial things such as what color dress Iris should have on and who should read the eulogy and various other unimportant things, had everyone's feathers ruffled, including Celeste. Poor Tom got lost somewhere in between "this is my child and Iris would have wanted us to . . ." After being questioned by several relatives as to whether or not he had insurance on Iris or if Iris had insurance, Tom chose to stay in a nearby hotel. All the chaos and confusion had just about converted NaNe's otherwise tranquil, serene abode into a literal hell hole.

Dante was ecstatic to have his nostrils greeted with an aroma of onions, cumin and garlic when he strolled into the house. Celeste had Ron Kenoly's "God Is Able" tape blaring from the speakers and hadn't heard him come in. His sudden appearance startled her so much that she dropped the cast-iron fryer back on the stove.

"Dante you scared me," she frowned.

"I'm sorry baby," he said kissing her on the cheek. The small kitchen was full of morning sun shimmering through the tiny window and bouncing off the glass table. The smell of fried potatoes and salmon cakes intoxicated Dante.

"Something sure smells good in here," he beamed lifting the top off one of the pots.

"Wash your hands," Celeste ordered popping him lightly with the dish cloth, a habit she picked up from many years of witnessing NaNe do it to her grandfather.

"You know Ms. Lady? We're going to have to do something about you being so bossy," he smiled.

"Whatever you think you need to do, baby. All I know is you better wash your hands before touching the food mister," Celeste repeated placing her hands on her hips.

"Yes ma'am," Dante said saluting her.

"Get out of here, Dante," she giggled. "You should go and take your shower. Breakfast will be on the table when you come out."

"All right," he agreed. "You okay?"

"I'm fine, for now. Just go do your thing. We can't be late."

Dante didn't reply. Instead he kissed her

on the forehead, turned sharply on his heels and walked toward the bathroom. Inside, he removed the rubber band from around the paper. The first page of the paper provided him with information about U.S. and Russian business relationships, increased mortgage rates and numerous other little articles. He whipped through the first few pages in less than five minutes before turning to the local section of the newspaper. Instantly, he lifted the paper closer to his face. The heading read: *Delivery truck driver who ran over girl found dead. Suicide or Homicide? Police still unsure.* Dante skimmed the article over hurriedly looking for clues that would link the driver to Iris. Mid-way through the article, he spotted the name Iris Dunbar and felt a rush of adrenaline kick in.

Now what the hell? he mumbled under his breath cringing his eyebrows. He let the paper topple to the floor as he gaped at the navy blue shower curtain. Right away, he knew that things were dangerously out of control. Visions of he and Celeste escaping to Tortola, where the blue waters and rich sand would be there only companions, were becoming very real. Knowing Celeste would be checking to see what was taking him so long, he quickly flipped on the shower, undressed and stepped in. Until he found out what was going on, no one seemed safe. Especially if Iris' death wasn't an accident and the delivery driver's death was a homicide. He would have to keep a sharper eye on Celeste today. *Hopefully*, Dante wished to himself, *Franchesco Gumichi would choose to pay his respects to his cousin Tom via telegram and not make a guest appearance. Either way he's going down soon*, Dante vowed. *Either way.*

Everyone arrived at NaNe's house by 10:30am. The block was lined with at least thirty cars when Dante, Celeste, Tom, NaNe and Uncle Deak came outside. Most of the family members were outside waiting for the procession to the funeral home to line up. There were somewhere between fifty to seventy five people loitering about in the streets and sidewalks or propped up against their cars. When the limousine driver stopped in front of the house, Aunt Joyce ran up to the car and started to get in. Uncle Deak was the first person to reach the car with NaNe following immediately behind.

Uncle Deak lightly held Aunt Joyce by the arm, preventing her from getting into the limo. "Joyce," Uncle Deak said lowly. "This car is for us," he said nodding his head over his shoulder toward NaNe, Tom, Celeste and Dante.

"Oh," Aunt Joyce said backing away from the car.

Celeste could tell Aunt Joyce's feelings were hurt at not being able to ride in the family car with Uncle Deak and NaNe, but there just wasn't enough room for everybody. Celeste thought about the eulogy she was supposed to deliver at the funeral parlor. She let out a deep breath trying hard not to focus on the emptiness she was feeling inside. Today, she would have to be strong, be vigilant. If not for herself, then definitely for NaNe and Uncle Deak.

At the funeral home everyone crowded into the left half of the funeral parlor while another service took place on the opposite side of the building. The walls in the tiny room, which surrounded the many relatives and acquaintances, began to sweat. After Celeste read the eulogy, she watched NaNe and Uncle Deak. NaNe had fainted for the second time in three days while Uncle Deak walked around in denial. Tom was the only one who did not outwardly display his emotions. He was scheduled to return to Europe tonight and made it obvious that he would wait until he arrived home to grieve for Iris. The way the family had carried on about the funeral arrangements Celeste couldn't blame him.

Dante motioned for Celeste to come and wait outside with him for the rest of the family. She spoke very few words to him in the limo and even fewer once they were outside alone.

"You all right?" he asked wrapping his arms around her slender shoulders.

"I'm trying," she faintly replied. "I'll be glad when this is all over."

"I know, darling," he reassured pulling her

closer while scanning the crowd for any signs of Gumichi and his pals. He had to be more attentive to their surroundings today. If only he could have gotten more information about the truck driver that turned up dead. Maybe then he would know for sure if indeed Celeste's life was in danger. Dante was working feverishly with the Bureau trying to gather as much information as possible on Tom, the dead truck driver and Mr. Gumichi. Dante let out a sigh which grabbed Celeste's attention.

Looking up at him with her large brown eyes, she managed a smile and said, "You know, you've been so preoccupied with me and my emotions I haven't even considered how stressful this must be for you. Are you okay?"

Dante's face brightened with a wide grin. He couldn't believe that even at a time like this Celeste still found a way to be concerned about someone else's well-being. "Don't worry about me. I'm here for you."

Luckily, the ceremony at the grave site went by swiftly and the body wasn't lowered into the ground while the family was there. While walking back to the car, Dante noticed that Tom had drifted off to the other side of the grave site. He strained hard from a distance in an attempt to see who the men were talking to Tom. Everything about them oozed malevolence. He was fairly certain that the man facing him directly was Fran-chesco. But then again, he couldn't be too sure from his vantage point. Right now the only true issue was returning back to NaNe's house and mapping out a course of action. Even with Alvin out of the picture, Gumichi was still hell bent on setting an example or making some kind of statement. He was sure that by now, Franchesco had to know that Alvin had flipped on him. What he couldn't figure out was what Franchesco really wanted. If only the diskettes would have provided more information that would stick to Gumichi, his little butt wouldn't even be here now. But Franchesco was careful and smart. No wonder he trusted Alvin and his missing nephew to do the job. Franchesco figured if they screwed up, he would make sure that nothing would stick to him. From everything Alvin had told him, that was all there was to it. A failed attempt to inter-link some names from the DEA and the FBI files to that of Gumichi's information. Nothing more to it supposedly, or was there? Dante wondered.

Dante could feel his heartbeat starting to kick in once the driver pulled out of the cemetery. Gumichi was up to something, he determined. But what?

Alvin stared out of the small bay window allowing the sunrays to penetrate his skin. Out of all the places in America he could have relocated to, Arizona was the selected place. He had spent the last few weeks getting acclimated to his new environment and identity. *Peter Winston, what a pitiful name for a brother,*

he thought frowning. He preferred Alvin
Brouchard, the engineer, much more so than
Peter Winston, the store manager of the local
hardware store. And even much more than
that, he would rather have a computer and a
modem so that he could have contact with the
outside world. But the Bureau wouldn't allow
it. They made sure that he was isolated from
any form of communication. The little town
had no fax machines, no cellular phones, no
computers and no damn ATM's. It was a little
ghost town with a population of 11,000, of
which only 100 or so were black folks. The
women were unpolished, the men chubby and
the radio stations hideous. Perhaps he should
have remained in DC and stood up to Gumichi and his goons instead of choosing to
reside in purgatory for the remainder of his
living days.

Alvin let his mind run back to that night
with Tony. Leaning back on the kitchen chair,
he let out a deep breath and began reminiscing. Basically, the choice was made and now it
was too late to undo the damage. The FBI
would crucify him if he attempted to disappear from the program now, especially once
they realized that he had pulled the wool over
their eyes. Actually, there was no $150,000. Or
real diskettes that posed a threat to Gumichi.
Sure there was some vital information that Gumichi shared with him to see if they could
devise a method for weeding out informants
via modem information. But that wasn't what

Gumichi was after him and Tony for. Tony was smart to drop out of sight and take the loot, Alvin thought quietly. The only mistake Tony made was taking everything. The loot totaled over half a million dollars, plus the suitcase of cocaine that had an estimated street value of two million dollars. "Greedy son of a bitch," Alvin huffed aloud. "He should have left some for me."

Alvin closed his eyes and reminisced about that dreadful evening with Tony. Everything had gone according to plan that night they stopped to meet the head of the Portrello family. Tony had the suitcase filled with the stuff while Alvin sat behind the driver seat. After the exchange took place and everyone checked their suitcases to make sure everything was in order, Tony, having had one too many beers and too many puffs on a homemade cigarette, panicked when he heard a noise coming from the alley. A damn alley cat rattling the garbage cans was the cause of all this crap that he was in. With Tony being buzzed and incoherent, he didn't think, he just reacted by pulling out a gun, which he had hidden from Alvin, and emptied it out on the two Portrello brothers. Scared and zooming, Tony grabbed both suitcases, jumped in the car and then they sped off. He promised to settle everything with his uncle in the morning. That's the only reason why I let him crash at my place, Alvin reasoned. After waking up in the morning and noticing Tony and the suitcases were gone, then having Gumichi's thugs looking for him, Alvin knew Tony had not followed through on his promise to settle things with his uncle. Word from the druglords on the street had it that some big time, discreet, dealer from Europe was pissed about not receiving his shipment and was planning on a trip to the States to settle up the score. It never dawned on him that anything more than what he was hired to do was going down. He realized now that the diskettes were just a side job to test his sense of loyalty. Once Franchesco saw his faithfulness, he would be trusted to go with Tony to make this important transaction.

Gazing out the window at the hundreds of cactus plants, Alvin let more air escape through his nostrils. He knew he had to let someone know the truth because Celeste's life was still in danger. For no other reason than the fact Gumichi wants to punish me and send a message. It's all about teaching a lesson, making an example with those guys. How could he reach Celeste to let her know? How could he protect her when he was so far away? Why should he want to protect her? She left him to die out there on the streets, refusing to return his calls. Besides, she's been sleeping with the enemy, Dante. So why should he care what happens to her? Perhaps because he didn't want anything to happen to an innocent bystander, even if it was Celeste.

Alvin thought about Dante and the witness protection program he had provided for him based on the information he had given him.

There was no way he could get in touch with Dante. Not now. It could mean being tossed out of the witness protection program if Dante found out the truth. Alvin wondered where Tony was and what alias he had assumed to protect his identity from his uncle and the government. He wanted to know what country Tony had escaped to and whether or not he would ever be caught?

"All that money and that bastard got away free," Alvin said rolling his eyes to the back of his head. He let out a final, deep sigh then mumbled, "God please. Don't let anything happen to Celeste because of me." The prayer had been sent up. He just hoped that Gumichi would let it drop because there was nothing else that could be done, or was there?

The tears had subsided by the time the limo pulled in front of NaNe's house. Celeste entered the house and headed straight upstairs to the bathroom. The rest of the family members, crowded into the house behind her like a herd of sheep being wrestled about. Dante stayed downstairs glancing upstairs occasionally to keep an eye on Celeste's whereabouts. NaNe walked into the kitchen, flipped on the kettle then walked outside onto the back porch where she sat down at the small card table. Mother Williams and Big Ma joined her shortly deciding that it would be better if she was in the company of someone other than herself.

Mr. Ted, Uncle Deak's neighbor and his wife and eldest daughter, gathered on the sofa in the living room. Cousin Charlotte and Aunt Ruthie began placing the food out and setting the table while Uncle Sammie, Cousin Bobby and Aunt Joyce saw to it that the bottles of liquor they brought with them stayed less than full as they poured themselves another drink and gobbled it down. A few of Uncle Deak's co-workers, and other stray relatives found places to rest.

"Where's Little Bit?" Uncle Deak asked sipping on a glass of gin, something he rarely did.

"She's upstairs," Dante replied somberly, knowing deep in his heart the day's events had not ended.

Seventeen

Currently . . .

Celeste woke up from her incoherent state when the black four-door sedan finally came to a halt. The blindfold was still wrapped tightly around her eyes preventing her from seeing her surroundings. She heard one of the men open the car door and mutter something to a man seemingly outside the car. Still groggy from the effects of the drug, Celeste was tongue-tied as she blurted, "You guys have made a mistake. You have the wrong person."

The men purposely ignored her statement while they helped her out of the car.

"Where are you taking me?" Celeste gasped. "Tell me what this is all about."

The men led her to a room filled with cigar smoke, choking Celeste upon her entrance. Celeste was forced to take a seat on the sofa. She let her hands roam across the cover of the sofa and knew immediately that it was made of a fine, soft leather. The carpet was thick and plush as her shoes sank into it further. She could feel someone watching her from across the room and determined that he was the person responsible for the room smelling the way it did. Celeste also could tell that whoever it was staring at her from across the room had a drink in his hands because she could hear the ice cubes clinking against the side of the glass.

She could hear the person in the room moving closer and closer to her side of the room. She could feel her heartbeat picking up its pace again as she took a deep breath attempting to contain its pace. Celeste heard the pinching sound of a leather chair and knew that the other person had decided to take the seat across from her. Leather furniture had a certain sound to it whenever someone sat down on it. There was another stint of silence before the person sitting opposite her spoke.

"Can I get you anything?" the man asked.

Celeste paused for a moment before speaking. She was thinking about how to reply to such an inappropriate and ridiculous question. Her heart was pounding out of control while she wondered who the person was talking to her. What she really wanted to say, rather scream, was *let me go please!* Instead, she kept silent hoping that her lack of response would help her foe realize that what he was asking was nothing short of idiotic.

"Well," the man started in a husky tone, "I suppose you're wondering why you're here."

No, Celeste smirked internally. *It's everyday that I'm snatched from a street corner against my will, blindfolded, drugged and whisked across town.*

Still Celeste did not reply. She sat stiffly with an arched back and a perfectly straight head.

Franchesco admired her resilience although it was beginning to annoy him. He took another sip from his glass, swallowed hard, crossed his legs and stated, "It appears that there has been some type of communication breakdown with one of our mutual friends. I was hoping you could fill in the gap for me."

Celeste let out an obvious sigh of frustration before replying, "I've already told those men that I don't know who you are or what it is you're looking for."

"I want Alvin Brouchard," Franchesco said angrily.

Celeste knew right off by the man's response that indeed she was sitting before the notorious Franchesco Gumichi. Who else would have done this to her? Keeping her facial expression even she responded, "What about him? We haven't been together in over six months," she said softly trying to disguise the nervousness in her voice.

"Really?" Franchesco genuinely replied. "And you haven't heard anything from him since that time?"

Celeste thought about his question before answering. Matter of fact, she hadn't heard from him in a few weeks. Not since Labor Day weekend when he had the altercation with Dante at the ice cream parlor. Clearing her throat, she strained to speak. "May I have a glass of water please?"

"Certainly. After you answer the question."
He was leaning forward on the edge of the
sofa, closer to her now.

"I haven't spoken to Alvin in several weeks
now. Like I said before, we are not seeing one
another anymore."

Franchesco left her presence for a brief moment, then returned with a glass of water.
Placing it in her hand he continued with the
questioning. "What did he talk to you about
when you spoke with him last?"

"Nothing really," she said pausing to take a
sip of her drink. "Something about us getting
back together. He was drunk."

Franchesco leaned back against the sofa eyeing her intensely. *She was lying.* He knew that
Alvin was not the begging type. He had too
much pride, too much confidence. He picked
up the cigar that had been left burning in the
ashtray, took a long drag then let the smoke
escape toward Celeste's direction. He eyed Celeste as she yanked her head to the left in an
attempt to avoid the smoke. Franchesco was
sure that Alvin had probably contacted Celeste
for help. What he wasn't sure about was if she
gave him the assistance he needed to pull off
the stunt. Sitting the cigar back down in the
ashtray, Franchesco got up and walked across
the room. Staring out over the balcony, a habit
for him whenever he had to sort things out,
he let out another long breath. He was really
hoping that snatching this girl would not be
in vain. Surely he didn't want to have another

meaningless murder on his hands, especially without gathering the necessary information he desperately needed. There was somebody else he had to answer to immediately and he needed the information tonight!

Dante rushed out the door and down the block when the neighbor entered NaNe's house with the news about Celeste being snatched. Looking up and down the street frantically, he returned to the house. Everyone was gathered around on the porch when he returned.

"What happened Dante?" NaNe panicked.

"I don't know yet. Excuse me," he said rushing past her into the house. Grabbing the telephone he punched in a few numbers. The voice on the other end picked up on the second ring.

"This is KODY, meet me at the spot in ten minutes. The sons of bitches snatched Celeste. We've got to go get her now!" Hanging up the phone, Dante turned abruptly to find NaNe and Uncle Deak standing behind him.

"What the hell is going on around here, Dante?" Uncle Deak said glaring at him. "Who was that you were talking to just now? And who the heck is KODY?"

NaNe said nothing. She just stood there with a look of shock like she was ready to go into cardiac arrest. Uncle Deak was beginning to get physical now with Dante, grabbing him by his arm. "Listen, Dante I want some answers and I want them right this minute!"

Dante shook his arm free from Deak's hand and answered, "I don't have time to explain it now. I've got to go save Celeste." Facing Deak, Dante put a hand on his shoulder for reassurance. "Trust me, Uncle Deak, NaNe," he said acknowledging her too. "I will not let anything happen to her. I promise."

"To hell with promises. I'm coming with you," Uncle Deak threatened.

Dante looked at him and shook his head. "I'm sorry, I can't let you do that. It could jeopardize everything."

At Dante's comment, NaNe stepped in and said in a raised voice, "Jeopardize what? What in God's name are you talking about? Where is Little Bit? What has happened to her?"

Dante could feel his patience wearing thin. He was trying hard not to disrespect Uncle Deak and NaNe but they were making it difficult. Scratching his head he raised his voice and spouted in a slow, even voice, "I do not have time to go into it. Every minute I waste trying to console you is another minute of time lost for Celeste. What I need is some co-operation here."

But NaNe and Uncle Deak didn't budge. They just stood determined to block his exit until he answered their questions satisfactorily. NaNe was the first to speak. "How come you know so much about what's going on? Are you mixed up in something that has put my baby in trouble, Dante? 'Cause if you did," she warned moving closer to him with balled fists,

"I'll kill you myself. We've already lost one of our children, a second one for me, and I swear before God we will not lose Celeste too."

Dante took a deep breath as Tom and the other family members were starting to gather behind her. It was the Dunbar clan for sure, he thought looking past her shoulder at the faces of the other relatives, who were beginning to comment as well. "Call the police," someone advised from the group.

"Yeah," commented everyone in unison.

"Listen up everyone," Dante ordered in a firm voice trying once again to get through the kitchen and to the front door. He had managed to make it halfway to the front door before continuing. "Nothing is going to happen to her. Now please just relax as best you can until you hear from me. There is no need to call the police. I will take care of it. Just let me go take care of my business."

"Why? Who are you that we should trust you?" Aunt Joyce instigated.

"That's right," Uncle Bobbie said stepping up to him at 5'7 like he wanted to scrap.

"Because I'm a FBI agent. That's why. Now let me go do my job."

"What?" NaNe said placing her hand on her hip. "You're what? How come you never said anything before? Does my granddaughter know? Did you at least tell her?" NaNe was fuming with anger. How could this boy keep something like that hidden? How could he have sat at the edge of her bed, looked in her eyes and assured her that he wasn't hiding anything when she had asked him? How?

The rest of the family members fell silent, while several bottom lips dropped at Dante's unexpected news. Shocked, the Dunbar clan moved to the side, making a path so that Dante could reach the front door. Tom eyed Dante for a long while, then turned away and walked out the kitchen to the backyard. NaNe and Uncle Deak stared at Dante with widened eyes. Too many things were unfolding in their lives too rapidly, NaNe quietly assessed.

Time was ticking away and Celeste had to be found. NaNe strangled her temptation to continue questioning Dante about his well-kept secret. Uncle Deak leaned back against the wall also trying to refrain from further questioning. *How was he able to pull his dual identity off?* he wondered but did not ask. All he knew was that Dante had better not be the reason Celeste was kidnapped.

Dante opened the front door and swiftly left the house. He had wasted too much time already with Celeste's stubborn family members. If anything happened to her, he would never forgive himself for not watching over her more carefully and allowing her to leave the house without him. Nor would he forgive Alvin Brouchard for that matter. As a matter of fact, he thought to himself as he started the car, *if anything did happen to Celeste, Alvin could kiss his damn life good-bye as well.*

Dante swirled the 300ZX around the corner

stopping abruptly in front of the lady sitting in a blue Ford Taurus. "Jump in!" he yelled through the window. Quickly the woman jumped in the car with a large duffle bag. Before she had time to shut the car door, he had sped off again.

"What's happening, KODY?" Leslie Cooper said looking at Dante. She was one of the special agents from the Philadelphia branch working with him to unravel the syndicate in the D.C. area as well.

"Gumichi got to Celeste," he spewed, eyes never leaving the road.

"How?" she queried pulling the heavy, black, steel vest from out of the bag and laying it on her lap.

"From the corner down the street from her house," Dante frowned as he punched the pedal harder till it reached 85 mph. "Gumichi has lost his damn mind. Did you call for back up to meet us at Gumichi's?"

"Yeah. They'll be there."

"They know to wait until we get there right?" Dante quizzed.

"I told them to sit tight."

"Good," he mumbled clutching the steering wheel tighter as he hugged the curve. "If they go at it too soon we could lose her."

There was a brief moment of silence until the sounds of magazine clips filled with bullets clicked into place. Dante struggled to keep control of the car with his knees while Leslie assisted him with his bullet proof vest. Another moment of quietness loomed in the air until Leslie uttered a question.

"I don't understand this KODY. What does Celeste have to do with all this?"

"She used to be Alvin Brouchard's old flame. I don't know, maybe Gumichi's sending a message."

"Yeah but why? He has to know that Alvin has handed the diskettes over to us by now. So what difference does it make to Gumichi if he sends a message or not? You and I both know we don't have enough crucial evidence on the diskettes to put him away forever. The best we could do is hold him temporarily for tampering with government records. And that probably won't even stick. Surely, he must know that too."

"Maybe, but why would he snatch Celeste unless the diskettes can provide incriminating information? I think we need to take a look at the diskettes again. Maybe we missed something. Or maybe Alvin has left out a crucial part to this puzzle."

"Yeah but what? It just doesn't add up KODY," Leslie said shaking her head looking out over the Potomac. "It just doesn't."

Celeste was given a choice to stay blindfolded with her hands remaining tied, or without the blindfold with her hands and feet tied. She chose to see the light. Gumichi had taken a slight liking to her and her feisty spirit. She sat in the room adjacent to the large family room peering out the large window. Her mind began sifting through information and previous conversations in an attempt to help her understand her current predicament.

Alvin must have done something terribly underhanded to drive Gumichi to this point, she reasoned. Gumichi had a soft look about him, even when he appeared disgruntled. She couldn't imagine him causing bodily harm to anyone himself. But then again, she was certain that he didn't gather his well-known reputation by being an altar boy.

The sky had opened up for the third time today as the water poured down and drenched everything exposed to it. Celeste's mind switched back to her captors and their alleged dealings with Alvin. *What the hell did he do, or not do to cause Gumichi's henchmen to snatch her? What or who would get her out of this mess? Where the heck has Alvin been anyway? Why didn't they snatch him?* The questions overpowered all other thoughts, except of Dante's face as he had motioned to her from across NaNe's living room to wait a minute earlier that day.

Her wrists were beginning to itch from the rope wrapped around them. Tired of sitting in the same position, she tried to slouch back against the loveseat and elevate her feet atop the coffee table. The hours ticked by as she prayed a rescue angel would come her way.

Eighteen

Dante pulled the car over to the curb behind the telephone repair truck, which was parked two houses down the street from Franchesco Gumichi's mansion. Grabbing the duffel bag, he glanced over at Leslie and commanded, "Let's go."

Two men dressed in Bell Atlantic jackets jumped out of the repair van and met Dante and Leslie midway through their stride up the street. Falling in line two wide and two deep, everyone concentrated on the goal, which was to save Celeste no matter what the cost.

"What you got?" Dante said eyeing one of the men.

"The house doesn't appear that full. Two guards are casing the grounds and Franchesco and his lieutenant, Nikko, seem to be the only heavies in the house. We're pretty sure the girl is in the house too."

"Fine work," Dante said lifting the gun to the side of his face near his ear as they approached the gate. "Any dogs?" he whispered.

"Hadn't noticed any," one of the men replied.

"Good! I hate dogs. Let's roll," Dante said assessing the gate once more, then letting his eyes roam back to the street. He had to be sure that no one would foil their attempt before they had a chance to implement the plan. He noticed a large car slowly rolling to a stop in front of the house across the street. He couldn't make out the person behind the wheel. But he could feel someone watching him. Deciding that saving Celeste was much more important than addressing the person in the boxy car, he turned his back and concentrated on what lay ahead of him.

It surprised Dante that Gumichi had not secured his premises with a little more iron. Matter of fact, this was feeling a bit too easy as Dante and Leslie, along with the back up men, climbed over the top of the gate with the help of the fifteen foot pine tree. *This is way too easy*, Dante surmised once his feet hit Gumichi's property. *No dogs, no wired fences, no nothing.* Before Dante had a chance to react to his gut feeling, the bush-hidden flood lights surrounding the grounds came to life as the backyard lit up like Candlestick Park at night. Immediately, everyone shielded their eyes trying to fend off the bright, sharp, unexpected lights.

"Throw your hands up!" demanded a voice from afar as a gunshot warning rang in the air. Dante fought hard to keep his position as did his comrades by shadowing their foreheads with one arm to block out the light and aiming their weapons with their free hand. But the second gunshot was not a warning. Instead, it pierced the blue jeans of one of the other men, hitting him in the knee. The man screamed and fell to the ground hard as the voice repeated, "Don't make me ask again. Now throw your hands up!"

"FBI!" Dante screamed, but it was too late. A third shot rang out drowning out Dante's statement. He ran for cover, diving into a pile of azalea bushes while Leslie followed behind. The second man lay holding his shoulder not far from the first man.

"Damn!" Dante huffed. "I knew it was too damn easy." He threw a glance at Leslie who was behind the bushes assessing their escape pattern.

"There's a clearing over in that area," she said nudging Dante.

Dante didn't reply or follow her finger. He was engrossed in thoughts of Celeste and her safety, her whereabouts. Finally, Dante locked eyes with Leslie and whispered, "I'll cover for you. Go and get more backup. I can't leave Celeste in there. I've got to save her!"

Leslie gave Dante a disapproving look but didn't express her thoughts. Instead, she scurried alongside the tall trees toward the back area. Dante watched anxiously until he saw her clear the fence over to the opposite side.

Leslie raced to the van, nearly knocking over a tall man, dressed in a long overcoat with his hands tucked in his pockets, walking toward her on the sidewalk. "Excuse me," she muttered faintly, as the man's eyes followed her movements to the van then focused back to the large mansion before him. Placing his left foot on the bottom step, he looked over at his car parked across the street to make sure he had turned off the headlights. First gunshots and now this. *Stuff was getting out of hand inside this house,* he summarized, and turned to walk up the steps. But he was here to set everything straight. He was sure of it, he promised reaching the top of the steps then pressing the doorbell. This would be the night to clear the air.

Dante took a deep breath then crouched back down behind the bushes. Leslie would phone for backup and the house would be infested with FBI agents in a matter of minutes. He had to think fast if he was going to save Celeste before it was too late. Cautiously popping his head above the bushes, he honed in on his two crew men who lay helplessly in the middle of the large yard. Just as he was about to squat back down for cover, he felt a presence behind him. *Awh, hell,* he remembered thinking before a metal object crashed down across the back of his head.

"Tom," Franchesco bellowed, with great surprise and uneasiness, as he greeted his cousin in the foyer. "What are you doing here? I thought you were on your way back to Europe tonight."

"I needed to come by and say good-bye once more before making the long trip," Tom replied walking past him toward the picturesque patio. "This is a beautiful place you have here Franchesco. You've done good for yourself. Your daddy would be proud."

Franchesco signaled Nikko with a quick nod then turned to face his cousin. "Yes Tom I think you're correct. Father would have been impressed. Here," he said, placing a hand on his shoulder, then guided him over to the sofa. "Have a seat. Can I get you something to drink?"

"Do you have cognac?" Tom asked tailing behind Franchesco. He didn't feel much like sitting down. His adrenaline was starting to kick in.

"Sure," Franchesco replied dryly. "Go ahead and have a seat and rest your coat."

"I'm fine really. I won't be staying long. I've got to get to the airport soon," Tom responded looking around the family room. "So, how many rooms are in this place?"

"Thirteen," Franchesco said handing him the glass. "Lucky number thirteen. How did you say you found me?" Franchesco wasn't feeling particularly in the hosting mood. He had a series of dilemmas facing him and knew that his time was limited. Hell, with a hostage across the hall and two men down in his back yard and another one on his way in the house, he really didn't care much about being hospitable.

"How about a tour of the house?" Tom insisted.

Franchesco's pupils widened at his cousin's

sudden request. This whole thing was starting
to feel peculiar to him. What was Tom doing
here in the States anyway? Franchesco frowned.
Tom's footsteps clanking against the hard wood
floors in the foyer snapped him out of his reverie.

"Hold on a second," he said, halting Tom's
steps. "Let me grab a glass of cognac and then
give you the tour. The house is so big, you
know?" Franchesco smiled. What he was really
trying to do was buy some time for Nikko and
the others to move Celeste and the intruder
to another part of the house. Tom could sense
that Franchesco was stalling and tried to get
a handle as to why? After a few minutes,
Franchesco made his way back across the room
to where Tom stood.

"Don't you want to take your coat off?"
Franchesco asked. "We've got a lot of ground
to cover."

"I'm fine, thank you. Like I said, I just
dropped by to say farewell before leaving.
That's all," Tom said grinning.

"I see. Well then, we better get started. Are
you ready for the grand tour?" Franchesco
asked.

"More than you know," Tom smiled as he
smoothed his hand over the metal object in
his left pocket.

"Move it!" Nikko threatened tossing Celeste
in the mauve-colored wall papered room then

closing the door behind them. "Sit down and keep your mouth shut," he instructed pushing her down in a chair then wrapping additional rope around her wrist and intertwining it with the back of the chair. Then he took a white cloth and tied it around her mouth. "Just sit still! We'll be back for you sooner than you can count to a thousand. Seems like someone attempted a rescue on your account. But don't worry, you're not going anywhere," Nikko smiled as he walked out the room.

Celeste let the tears flow down her cheeks again. How did all this happen? A few minutes had elapsed before the door to the room opened again. Even with her eyes puffy from all the tears she had shed, she could still see clearly. Clear enough to know that the man that Nikko and the other grunt tossed on the bed, with his hands tied behind his back, was Dante Lattimore.

She waited until the men had left and the door was shut before she attempted to scream Dante's name. The sounds were muffled because of the gag. For the next few seconds, she cried out to Dante through the cloth until he came to.

Still foggy from the blow across his head, Dante eventually held his focus long enough to recognize Celeste sitting across from him. He lifted his head a bit more to level it with hers and with squinted eyes groggily uttered, "Celeste, is that you?"

Celeste shook her head fiercely while muttering, "Yes."

"Hold on, sweetheart. I'll get you out of here," he reassured trying to wiggle free. But the rope binding his hands and ankles were tighter than normal. Closing his eyes, he concentrated on something pleasant, letting his body relax with each breath. After a few minutes of deep breathing and visualization, Dante managed to squirm loose one of his hands. A few seconds more, both hands were free as he worked viciously trying to undo the rope around his ankles. Flinging the ropes to the ground he rushed over to Celeste and immediately untied her gag.

"Dante," she breathlessly whispered while he worked quickly to untie the rest of her. "What are you doing here? How did you get here? Who . . . ?"

"Sshh," Dante said covering her mouth with his index finger. "I'll explain it later but first, I've got to get you out of here." He ran over to the window and peeked outside. The ledge was narrow and the drop at least two stories. Dante turned around and grabbed Celeste's hands and walked over to the door.

The only way out was through this door. The window was too high off the ground and chances were they'd be spotted right away. Suddenly, they could hear someone walking toward the room.

"Quick, over here," Dante mumbled pulling Celeste behind him and grabbing the vase full of flowers and water off the end table. Dante watched anxiously as the knob to the door turned slowly. The door creaked for a few seconds as Nikko swung it open wide, eyes searching for Dante and Celeste. Before he had a chance to brace himself, Dante slammed the vase across the back of his head. Water gushed everywhere as Nikko made his descent to the floor. Dante caught him before he crashed to the floor and dragged Nikko's broad body over to the bed where he began tying him up with rope. "Now you know how it feels," Dante uttered to an unconscious Nikko.

Pulling Celeste closely behind, Dante closed the door behind them and tiptoed down the long hallway and down a small set of steps toward what seemed like the front of the house. He knew if he could just reach somewhere safe, the backup units would be arriving anytime to assist them. They moved swiftly throughout the house trying to locate the front door. One more turn to the left and finally they were standing down the hallway with the front door facing them. The large family room sat adjacent to the front door which meant if anyone was in there, they would surely be found out. There was nowhere left to run, Dante assessed. They had to make it to the door. Turning, he faced Celeste and said, "This is it baby. The only thing standing between you and that door is me. If something happens to me, I want you to promise me you'll keep going and won't look back okay?"

"Dante no," she whispered with pleading eyes. "I won't leave without you. Please, let's both go for it."

"Celeste," he said stridently as he gently held her shoulders. "Understand what I'm telling you here. If something happens I want you to run out that door and down those front stairs. There'll be someone named Leslie waiting outside to help you. Just tell her that Gumichi is in the house by himself and that Nikko has been disarmed. All right?"

Celeste looked at him in wonderment. *What was he really doing here? And who the hell is Leslie? And how come he knows Nikko's name and that Gumichi is in the house alone?* She gave him a leveled gaze but said nothing. Dante was hell bent on saving her life no matter what she had to say about it. Moving closer to the family room and the front door, Dante could hear voices in the room. He stopped so suddenly causing Celeste to step onto the back of his heels. Celeste felt the breath of someone standing behind her. Slowly, she turned to face the short man holding a pistol to her head.

"Going somewhere?" the man grinned exposing his rotting teeth.

Dante turned around to see where the voice was coming from. He noticed that the pistol was pointed directly at Celeste's temple. *Damn!* Dante thought silently. It was one of the guards from outside. Within a few more seconds, Dante spun around to face the man tapping him on his shoulder. Dante knitted his eyebrows from disgust when his eyes locked with the man who had touched him on his shoulder. *So this is the notorious Franchesco Gumichi. Where the hell is the back up when I need them?*

Franchesco returned the half-cocked smile and motioned with his usual head nod to the man standing behind Celeste to whisk them away. But before he had a chance, Tom stepped out into the foyer to see what was going on. Tom gave Dante a quick head nod of his own as if to say don't acknowledge me. Celeste caught the gesture too and did not respond to Tom's unexpected appearance.

All the while Dante's mind was zooming with thoughts of betrayal, of set-up and deceit. How dare he pretend to be in mourning, better yet in love with Iris and the entire time working hand in hand with the Gumichis? How the hell could he do this? Who was this guy really anyway and why is he here? Dante had to bite his tongue to keep from spewing indecencies toward Tom.

"What's going on?" Tom said matter of fact-like as he put some distance between him and Franchesco.

"Nothing to concern yourself with, Tom. Why don't you go on back into the family room and let me take care of this situation," he hinted looking at Tom. In spite of Franchesco's growing tension lines in his forehead, Tom stood firmly in his pose: his back arched, shoulders broad, with his left hand in that left pocket.

The little man standing behind Celeste interrupted the silence by winking at Franchesco and stating, "I found them trying to jump over the back fence."

"That's a damn lie and you know it!" Dante flared.

"Now, now, mister, didn't you see that no trespassing sign posted on our gate outside? Do you know the penalty for trespassing onto somebody's else's property?" Gumichi said smiling.

Dante didn't bother to respond. Evidently, Franchesco was trying to save face in front of Tom, but why? Once again Franchesco motioned for the man to remove Celeste and Dante from the foyer. And once again Tom interrupted. "I say dear cousin. What's going on? Why do you think this man and this lovely lady would trespass onto your property? Looks like she's a little overdressed for that sort of thing," he said pointing to Celeste's dress with his right pointer finger.

Franchesco looked at Tom with angry eyes. "Let me handle this. Don't you have a plane to catch or something like that? Do you need me to get Nikko to take you to the airport? Nikko," Franchesco yelled. "Nikko, get down here now!"

"I'm afraid he's a little tied up at the moment," Dante said, eyeing Franchesco. "As a matter of fact, you're about to be fairly tied up yourself if you do something stupid," he continued. "You've done a lot of dumb things in your life Gumichi but offing a FBI agent would be pretty damn ultimate. What you think?"

"FBI?" Franchesco squealed with a raised brow. "I don't give a damn who you say you are. You were trespassing and that gives me the right to blow you away and toss you in the Chesapeake Bay if I want to. There's no way they'd be able to save you then, huh?" Franchesco laughed wildly. "You," he said pointing to the man standing behind Celeste. "Go upstairs and get Nikko."

As the man moved away to head up the stairs, Tom moved forward, cleared his throat and said, "I wouldn't do that if I were you."

"What?" Franchesco yelled turning hard to face Tom. Dante and Celeste inched toward the front door some more until they heard the man threaten them to stop. All Dante knew was that he was ready to get Celeste the heck out of there and didn't care what happened once he did.

"You heard me, cousin. I said that it would not be a good idea for him to go get that monstrous bodyguard of yours. We can handle this ourselves."

"Handle what? What exactly do you know about what's going on?"

"I know enough to not let him," Tom said pointing to the other man, "go upstairs and bring more problems downstairs."

"Listen, Tom. You're family and all but I swear, if you get in my way, if you cross me, I'll kill you myself."

"You mean you'd actually pull the trigger?" Tom snickered. "I don't believe it. Isn't that what your gooneys here do in order to keep you clean?" Tom was laughing louder now.

Franchesco cautiously backed away from Tom. How did his cousin know so much about him and his dealings? Just exactly what was his true purpose for being at his house tonight? Franchesco could feel his blood boiling at the thought of his own flesh and blood handing him over to the FBI.

"What's this Tom? You turning me in? Your own flesh and blood? Damn your soul for this Tom," he yelled.

With all the commotion going on, Dante took the moment to make a dash for the door with Celeste but stopped immediately when he heard the gunshot go off. Celeste screamed then covered her eyes. Spinning around slowly, Dante saw that the man had his gun pointed at Celeste. "Stay right there!" he ordered. "Mr. Gumichi, what you want me to do with them?"

But Franchesco was seething with rage as his eyes locked with his cousin turned enemy. After a few seconds, Gumichi turned to Louie and said, "Kill them. Kill them all."

Louie lifted the gun and pointed it directly at Celeste. Just then, Tom snatched his left hand out of his pocket and fired a shot into the shoulder blade of Louie.

Dante jumped in front of Celeste and pushed her down to the ground just as Louie's gun discharged in reaction to being shot by Tom. The dead weight of Dante's body crashing down on top of Celeste's body, along with the warm, wet liquid covering her hand, caused her to scream again.

"Dante! Dante. Oh my God!" she yelled hysterically with tears flowing from her eyes. She rolled Dante over onto his back using her leg as a pillow to hold his head. Rocking him back and forth, she cried frantically. Blood was oozing over her legs and hands. Trying to maintain her composure, she began talking to Dante. "It's going to be okay baby," she said sniffling. "Please hold on."

Meanwhile, Tom turned the gun toward his first cousin. Franchesco backed away slowly. Every thing was moving fast including his heart. *Where was Nikko? He should be handling this situation. That's what I pay him for,* Franchesco panicked silently. Gathering enough control in his voice he looked at Tom and mumbled, "Why are you doing this? Why?"

Tom glanced down at Dante then leaned back against the wall. He could feel the rage starting to build up in him for the first time since Iris' death. "For starters, let's just say you owe us. You didn't follow through and now you have to pay. You know what we mean by paying your debts, don't you, cousin?"

"What are you talking about Tom? Owe who? I don't owe you or anybody else for anything."

"Yes you do, cousin. You owe us about two million dollars in street value the way I see it."

"Two million dollars? Street value? You're

not making sense Tom," he said backing further into the family room.

"You know Franchesco, for that shipment we paid for but never received a few weeks ago, remember?"

Franchesco's face turned completely flush. *Could it be true? Could his cousin be the European connection that was expecting the shipment from the Portrello brothers that his nephew Tony and his friend Alvin stole? Ah Christ,* he thought letting out a deep breath.

"Oh, now you recall, don't you? See, I knew your memory wouldn't fail you especially with a .32 staring you in the face," Tom grinned while moving closer to Franchesco.

"I can explain that. It was her boyfriend, Alvin," Franchesco said raising his hand and pointing to Celeste. "He took your stash. Honestly. I sent them on the job and things got out of hand. I swear. Look, I can get your money. I have it in the safe."

"Too late for that now Franchesco. We shouldn't have had to come for it in the first place. But that's not what I'm so riled up about. I knew when I got on the airplane with my wife to come to the States that I was going to have to work things out. I fought long and hard with my people to try and convince them to spare you, my cousin's life. But when I found out that Iris' death was not an accident, well you know I just can't seem to forgive that one."

"My God, Tom! That was an accident. We were looking for her boyfriend, Alvin, and figured she was in on it or knew where the money and stuff was stashed. But I swear Tom, Iris was an accident."

"Save it, Franchesco. It's time to kiss me good-bye," he said walking over to his cousin and snatching him by the head with his right hand then placing the kiss of death on his lips. Franchesco tried to struggle but was too weak. Tom raised the gun to Franchesco's head right as the front door caved in.

Five people ran in and yelled, "FBI! Drop the gun! Now!" But it was too late. Tom squeezed the trigger and watched as Franchesco's forehead gushed open with blood before feeling a burning pain in his own upper chest. Tom had been shot by the FBI agents as he fell to the floor beside his cousin.

Celeste sat frozen with shock and rocking Dante back and forth. She couldn't believe what she had just witnessed. The paramedics immediately began CPR on Dante as Celeste stood by and watched the man she loved slipping away from her. If she lost one more person she loved, she would die herself. After seeing Dante's chest rise on its own, she let out a sigh of relief. She wanted to cry but didn't have any water left to spill. She thanked the Lord for sparing Dante's life as she watched the EMT's put the oxygen mask over his face then load him on the gurney.

Celeste hopped into the ambulance with Dante. Once inside the van, she took Dante's hand and held it tightly. He opened his eyes slightly and peered up at her over the mask covering his nose. He gave her a faint smile and returned the gesture by squeezing her hand back.

"I can't believe I almost lost you, Dante," she said reflecting on the evening's events.

"You won't lose me," he replied softly over the mask.

"You better not leave me. I love you too much," she smiled. "Besides, who would protect me if you left me here all alone?"

"I could never leave you. I want you with me always."

She took a moment to reply, before kissing his hair once more. "Then I guess you're my soulmate, Mr. Lattimore. I love you, Dante."

"Actually, I was hoping you were in need of a playmate as well," he chuckled faintly.

"Let's get you back in tip-top condition and then we'll see about all that," she grinned.

"Come closer," he directed as Celeste bent her head down till her ear almost touched his face. "I love you woman. Don't ever forget that for as long as we're together and even when we're apart. I'll always be there for you. Always."

"How do you know that Dante?" she teased.

"Because you're my soulmate," he said looking her squarely in the eyes. "Mine only."

Dear Reader,

I hope you enjoyed reading *HEARTS AFIRE* so much, that you were unable to do anything else because you had to finish this book! If that was the case, then you must pick up my first novel, *NO ORDINARY LOVE*. (WARNING: IF YOU'RE ALREADY SUFFERING FROM SLEEP DEPRIVATION, YOU MAY WANT TO CONTACT YOUR BED FOR A GOOD NIGHT'S SLEEP BEFORE INDULGING IN THIS BOOK!)

I'm interested in hearing what you have to say, *good* or *good*, about the characters and the storyline. You can submit your comments to:

Monique Gilmore
412 Southland Mall
Suite 201
Hayward, CA 94545

Thank you for your support. Spread the word!

ROMANCES ABOUT AFRICAN-AMERICANS!
YOU'LL FALL IN LOVE
WITH ARABESQUE BOOKS FROM PINNACLE

SERENADE   (0024, $4.99)
by Sandra Kitt

Alexandra Morrow was too young and naive when she first fell in love with musician, Parker Harrison—and vowed never to be so vulnerable again. Now Parker is back and although she tries to resist him, he strolls back into her life as smoothly as the jazz rhapsodies for which he is known. Though not the dreamy innocent she was before, Alexandra finds her defenses quickly crumbling and her mind, body and soul slowly opening up to her one and only love, who shows her that dreams do come true.

FOREVER YOURS   (0025, $4.99)
by Francis Ray

Victoria Chandler must find a husband quickly or her grandparents will call in the loans that support her chain of lingerie boutiques. She arranges a mock marriage to tall, dark and handsome ranch owner Kane Taggart. The marriage will only last one year, and her business will be secure, and Kane will be able to walk away with no strings attached. The only problem is that Kane has other plans for Victoria. He'll cast a spell that will make her his forever after.

A SWEET REFRAIN   (0041, $4.99)
by Margie Walker

Fifteen years before, jazz musician Nathaniel Padell walked out on Jenine to seek fame and fortune in New York City. But now the handsome widower is back with a baby girl in tow. Jenine is still irresistibly attracted to Nat and enchanted by his daughter. Yet even as love is rekindled, an unexpected danger threatens Nat's child. Now, Jenine must fight for Nat before someone stops the music forever!

Available wherever paperbacks are sold, or order direct from the Publisher. Send cover price plus 50¢ per copy for mailing and handling to Penguin USA, P.O. Box 999, c/o Dept. 17109, Bergenfield, NJ 07621. Residents of New York and Tennessee must include sales tax. DO NOT SEND CASH.